T0282681

THE MASTER PLAN

Raymond A. Hult

Order this book online at www.trafford.com
or email orders@trafford.com

Most Trafford titles are also available at major online book retailers.

© Copyright 2016 Raymond A. Hult.
All rights reserved. No part of this publication may be reproduced, stored in a
retrieval system, or transmitted, in any form or by any means, electronic, mechanical,
photocopying, recording, or otherwise, without the written prior permission of the author.

Print information available on the last page.

ISBN: 978-1-4907-7489-3 (sc)
ISBN: 978-1-4907-7493-0 (hc)
ISBN: 978-1-4907-7494-7 (e)

Library of Congress Control Number: 2016910769

Because of the dynamic nature of the Internet, any web addresses or links contained in
this book may have changed since publication and may no longer be valid. The views
expressed in this work are solely those of the author and do not necessarily reflect the
views of the publisher, and the publisher hereby disclaims any responsibility for them.

Any people depicted in stock imagery provided by Thinkstock are models,
and such images are being used for illustrative purposes only.
Certain stock imagery © Thinkstock.

Trafford rev. 07/05/2016

 www.trafford.com

North America & international
toll-free: 1 888 232 4444 (USA & Canada)
fax: 812 355 4082

INTRODUCTION

The plot of this novel centers on the theft of 1.5 million dollars by a sole armored car driver transporting the money from Utah to Nevada. I suspect readers will be inclined to disbelieve the premise an armored car company would allow such a transfer without a second driver to in part limit the temptation of such an embezzlement taking place. I would be the first to join in that skepticism had I not personally experienced that actually happening in real life.

I was stationed as a Special Agent with the FBI in St. George, Utah on July 16, 1996 when I got a call that a Wells Fargo Armored Car driver was missing along with $917,000 he was transporting from Utah to the main temporary storage facility in Las Vegas. It was soon determined the missing driver had made the trip by himself without a second driver. Outside foul play was initially suspected as those who knew the driver best were confident he would have never played a part in stealing the missing money.

I won't go into all the details of the investigation that ended with the driver finally being located and reluctantly admitting to me he had engineered the theft on his own despite relating to family and friends he had been kidnaped by two Mexicans and held captive until he was finally able to escape from Minnesota and return to Utah.

So, for any skeptics out there, the scenario in this book of a single driver is not only a realistically possibility, but I can personally confirm it actually happened in the summer of 1996.

ONE

"I, Samuel P. Donahue, having been informed of my rights as contained on an Interrogation, Advice of Rights Form, provide the following signed statement to FBI Special Agents David Hilton and Stephen A. Cook. The statement is free and voluntary on my part and I have not been coerced in any way to furnish it.

At approximately 3:30 pm on Friday, September, 24, 2014, I was robbed in the parking lot of Smith's Quick Stop in Mesquite, Nevada. I was returning to the armored car in which I was in the process of transporting $1, 501,023.67 consisting of bank receipts collected in Utah to the main Las Vegas, Nevada vault of United Liberty Inc. (UNI), an armored car service headquartered in Chicago, Illinois. I am the supervisor for the Southern District of Utah of UNI and, as had been required on rare occasions in the past due to a shortage of manpower, I was forced into making said delivery by myself without the normal second guard.

One of two robbers, a female, placed the barrel of a gun in the small of my back just as I was entering the armored car. She grabbed my keys and forced me across the seat to the passenger side where she slid over next to me. A second Mexican male almost simultaneously entered the armored car from the driver's side, took the keys from the female, and drove the armored car back toward the Utah border. I decided not to pull my gun because of the fear the female might pull the trigger with the barrel still buried into the left side of my waist.

It took about 10 minutes to cross the northwest corner of the Arizona border where we started traveling uphill in the Virgin River Gorge. We pulled off on what ended up being a deserted dirt road and traveled north for several miles finally stopping at an isolated spot where they had me get out and lay on the ground on my stomach. They took my weapon and had me stand and open the door where the money was being held. They then had me get back on the ground and told me they would shoot me if I looked up. They left in the direction from which we had come.

After a few minutes, I got up and started walking back toward the I-15. I was almost immediately able to hitch a ride with a truck driver who was headed east toward St. George, Utah. The driver dropped me off near the St George P.D. where I told Detective Brad Nelson what had happened. Unfortunately, I didn't get the name of the truck driver or bother to gather any additional information that may help identify him. I was too upset at that point to be thinking straight about anything except contacting the police.

It wasn't long after talking to detective Nelson that he called the St. George office of the FBI and Special Agents Hilton and Cook arrived at the police station and I agreed to furnish this statement.

Both suspects appeared to be Mexican and somewhere between 20 and 30 years old. It's possible they may have come from some other country south of the border. The male who didn't speak any English was about 5'6" and the female was several inches shorter. They both had dark brown hair and brown eyes. The male had pock marks all over his face and a tattoo of an eagle on his right forearm. The female was very pretty with smooth skin and wore a neckless with a gold cross around her neck. I think I could identify both of them if I saw them again. Both suspects were wearing gloves the entire time.

Neither of the suspects gave any indication of where they might be heading after they dropped me off. I know nothing about the circumstances of my armored car being located in the parking lot of the St George airport during the course of providing this statement. I had nothing to do with planning or executing the robbery.

I'm unwilling to take a polygraph to help prove my innocence. I know the results of such tests are notoriously unreliable and I see no benefit from subjecting myself when the possibility exists that such a test may falsely tend to incriminate me and distract from concentrating on the true suspects of this crime.

I have carefully reviewed and initialed both pages of this statement and certify that it is true and correct."

Sam signed the statement witnessed by both Hilton and Cook. The robbery would be investigated by the FBI since it had primary authority investigating bank robberies. The FBI also had jurisdiction regarding the Federal Interstate Transportation of Stolen Property Act which was obviously the case since the stolen money had crossed over both the Nevada and Arizona borders into Utah.

It was obvious the agents suspected him of stealing the money, but Sam was confident they wouldn't be able to prove he did it. He had been planning the theft for well over a year ever since he realized his tight-fisted employer had made a serious error in occasionally trusting him to transfer money to Las Vegas on his own when a second guard was unavailable. Sam had even warned his boss that they needed to hire another part-time employee for just such instances, but the boss had rejected the idea because he said UNI was cutting back on expenses.

Sam had planned on no longer being a UNI employee once his boss found out he had refused to take a polygraph test. He had no intention of going back to work now he had close to 1.5 million dollars at his disposal. He would simply tell his boss the theft had left him emotionally scarred to the point he wasn't willing to risk even the slightest possibility of such a harrowing event ever being repeated.

The die had been cast. There was no turning back now. He was fully committed to following through with no regret and an unwavering assurance derived from what he truly believed to be a meticulously conceived master plan imperious to failure.

TWO

Sam Donahue lived alone in a one bedroom apartment in St. George, Utah. Thirty eight years old, he was an only child. His parents had died in a car crash several years ago. He married his teenage sweetheart at age 19, but the acrimonious union lasted less than six years when his wife had an affair with and later married someone she met at the local gym. Luckily, they had no children to consider as fallout from of the divorce.

Most women were instantly attracted to Sam's dashing good looks and very few were hesitant about succumbing to any interest he might show them. He'd been reluctant to engage in any meaningful relationships after being stung on his first attempt. His dates mostly involved one night stands in bars located in the nearby gambling town of Mesquite, Nevada.

As a district supervisor for UNI, he had grown to detest his job. He was salaried and therefore got no extra pay for working as many as sixty or more hours per week. His regional supervisor in Salt Lake City was a penny pinching egotist who refused to add additional help to Sam's district to assist in easing the burden requiring him to all too often take on the roles of both supervisor and driver. When figuring in his unpaid overtime hours, he estimated he was earning less than $15/hr.

He wasn't about to try to justify his theft because of his less than ideal working conditions. He was a flat-out crook and willing to own up to the reality. He believed in the old adage "if you can't do the time, don't do the crime." If he got caught, he would try to negotiate a plea agreement that would hopefully minimize his time served or at least give him an opportunity to serve time in a low security federal prison camp housing the type of white collar convicts you didn't have to worry about bending over in the shower to pick up a bar of soap.

He had no previous criminal record and was clean as a whistle up until this point in time. He'd played by the rules his entire life and look where it got him. He'd advanced to a dead end job with little chance of turning things around. Thanks to what he blamed on a Republican controlled Congress, middle class employees like him were being ignored in favor of lobbyists interested more in the financial wellbeing of their wealthy employers than the plight of those of a lower class. Even middle-class college graduates were having difficulty finding decent employment. The likelihood of Sam finding anything better than his present dismal career was dubious at best. His supervisor was continually reminding him of that depressing reality.

Although willing to face the music if it came to it, he didn't plan on getting caught. He had been planning the heist for months on end and was confident he'd prepared for every possible contingency. The first rule of thumb he'd decided on was to make sure he was the only one who knew what he was up to. No one else who could identify him could be trusted with any element, no matter how small, of what he planned to do or any of the steps it would take to accomplish his devious charade.

He had seen enough TV shows and movies to conclude the slightest slip causing anybody to suspect he might be up to no good could prove disastrous. For that reason, any kind of suspicious activity his friends or associates might later be questioned about had to be avoided at all costs. Confidants who might at first appear unshakable about furnishing any comprising information needed to be kept completely in the dark.

It was for that reason he was wary about most conspiracy theorists. There were multiple reasons why most attempted conspiracies had a short life span. For example, a supposed trusted confederate often spilled the beans when he or she got in trouble and wanted to make a deal. There could be a falling out among partners in crime resulting in one or more associates wanting to get even. Divorced spouses and jilted lovers were probably the most risky of all. No, it was better not to trust anyone who might later be able to tie him to any of the details of his shrouded scheming.

Sam had done a lot of planning on his computer; especially, about what it would take to disguise his stolen cash so it couldn't be traced back to the theft. Several weeks before the alleged heist, he had buried the computer and its incriminating hard drive in a remote desert location where it could never be retrieved. Just to be sure, he had damaged the hard drive to the extent no damaging information could be retrieved even if it was someday dug up.

A search of his apartment, workplace and car would prove fruitless. There wasn't a single piece of evidence that could tie him to the crime or his ill-gotten gain. He wouldn't again talk about the theft to the FBI or anybody else for that matter. They had all the information they were going to get in the statement he had voluntarily signed. He would simply respond he was taking the advice of an unidentified attorney.

Too many suspects carelessly allow themselves to be subjected to extensive voluntary interrogations where they become disoriented and end up saying something stupid that can be used against them. Sam wasn't going to fall into that trap. He was confident any of the generalized information he had furnished in his statement would prove worthless in building a case against him.

Considering the impending risk, Sam confidently pondered: *Give it your best shot Mr. FBI man. Come at me from every angle in your arsenal. This is all I've been thinking about for over a year. I'm totally prepared for the long run. Time is on my side and my exhaustive preparation will eventually prevail over your investigative prowess.*

THREE

In the early evening hours after their interview, SAs Hilton and Cook were becoming more involved by the minute. Sitting in their newly furnished two-man Resident Agency (RA) on the third floor of a brand new office building in the middle of downtown St. George, Cook angrily speculated, "He stole the money and I think he knows we know he did it. Refusing to take a polygraph and any further interview isn't the way someone who's innocent normally reacts. It's like he's daring us to prove his guilt."

"I agree. The reality is, however, as I've experienced many times before, the chance of pulling off a perfect crime is extremely unlikely." SA Hilton, the Senior Agent in Charge of the RA and the more pragmatic of the two, often found himself trying to calm down his frequently more excitable junior first office agent. "I'm predicting our Mr. Donahue has already made or will soon make significant mistakes sinking his boat if he stole the money. It's not easy to steal and then hide a theft of that magnitude."

Cook nodded slightly although it was hard to determine if he was absorbing the sage assurance of his senior mentor. "Have you heard back from Salt Lake City yet about our request for some extra manpower?"

"Not yet," Hilton responded, "but I'm expecting a call from the Special Agent in Charge anytime now. He said he we would definitely be getting some help, but he wasn't sure how much or for how long until he talked to a couple of supervisors who weren't going to be ecstatic about diminishing their ability to handle their own already cumbersome caseloads. I expect whoever we end up getting will be on their way down here by late tonight or early tomorrow morning."

Steve wasn't thrilled about the possibilities. "If it's similar to our experience in the recent past, anybody we get is going to be on the bottom of the heap as far as their headquarter supervisors are concerned. They aren't going to willingly let any of their best help come down here; especially, if it's for any kind of extended period. I can tell you right now we're not going to be getting the pick of the litter."

"Oh ye of little faith," Dave cautioned. "I still think we've got a good shot at getting the premier surveillance squad for at least part of the time. Those guys are as good as it gets. I realize they're in high demand, but we're talking about a lot of money here. I think that may put us on the top of the list. What we need more than anything right now is quality 24 hour surveillance on every move Donahue makes. If he's temporarily stashed the money and/or he's involved in a conspiracy with anyone else, we need to be there when he incriminates himself. The surveillance squad will bring a high altitude plane that will make it easier to follow without spooking him. I want you to get over to Donahue's place right now and make sure he doesn't go anywhere. Call me if he does and I'll help follow. Otherwise, I'll stay here for the next few hours to coordinate with headquarters.

Less than an hour later, St. George was allotted use of the premier surveillance unit and its plane for the next seven days. They would be ready to set up at Donahue's residence or where ever else the St. George agents were able to place him by 5am the next morning. It took about 4 hours to drive from Salt Lake and they would be available to be briefed and develop a game plan sometime around midnight at the RA.

Dave loved his job, but he'd be turning 55 in a few more months and that would necessitate a mandatory retirement. The

FBI was strange that way. Agents were required to maintain their fitness for duty through regular firearms testing and yearly physical fitness exams. Steve's scores had remained high. He had gained valuable experience that would be missed. He figured he could go another five years or more with no loss in productivity. Nevertheless, rules were rules and he was rapidly approaching the end of a stellar career in which he had received numerous awards in recognition of his tireless efforts to go the extra mile.

The one good thing was the FBI retirement was generous. Dave could remain completely retired with no need to seek another job to supplement his annuity. All the kids had left the roost and appeared to be happily married and financially secure. Seven grandchildren had blessed their situation as proud grandparents. Dave and Pam had remained deeply devoted to each other since their youthful wedlock over thirty-five years ago. They especially enjoyed traveling together. The ability to significantly expand that passion while still young and healthy portended a unique and fortuitous opportunity.

Although never known for backing away from a challenge, Dave was kind of hoping his last few months would be relatively uneventful. That would allow him to better prepare for what was undoubtedly going to result in a major life style change. Besides, he was just starting to recover from an exhausting meth case involving public corruption on the part of the local County Sheriff. He had never worked less than a 50 hour week throughout his 25 year career, but he had been working far more than that until just recently when the Sheriff finally agreed to plead guilty.

The thought of going out like a lamb looked highly unlikely now. Samuel P. Donahue appeared ready to insure that wasn't going to happen.

FOUR

Binions Horseshoe in Las Vegas once had 1 million in cash on display in $100 bills. The tightly fitted display case was about 4 feet square and 18 inches high. Sam's load contained a variety of bill denominations in addition to some coin. In the end it had taken six 5 gallon air-tight and waterproof plastic drums with heavy duty handles to safely store and transport the bills. He left the coins behind. The drums would fit neatly into the trunk of his car. The net haul ended up totaling slightly over 1.5 million.

He purchased the containers several months earlier using cash at a Home Depot in North Las Vegas. He wore a baseball cap, sun glasses and an extremely realistic looking fake mustache in making the purchase. Shortly after the purchase, with the exception of the mustache, he discarded the clothes he was wearing that day along with the ball cap and cheap glasses used to hide his identity from the store's security camera. He made sure his car had been parked far enough away from the store's parking lot to escape any camera surveillance.

Of course, the chance that anyone would ever check that particular Home Depot to see if Sam had purchased drums was near zero. If everything went as planned, there would be no reason for law enforcement to even suspect that drums had been a part of the theft. Still, Sam was taking no chances. Even a near zero chance of detection was something to be avoided.

The mustache along with other sophisticated facial disguise materials had been previously purchased at a Hollywood, California specialty store that catered primarily to the movie industry. Even if law enforcement was lucky enough to subsequently discover his cache of face altering paraphernalia, his master plan allowed for a reasonable explanation that would provide a gambling reason for the gear unrelated to the robbery.

Sam had picked a spot behind the top of a ridge along the same dirt road where he had allegedly been cast aside by his captors. More than a week before, a hole had been dug where the drums could easily be inserted and covered up with large flat rocks to match the surrounding terrain and make it highly unlikely that any future search would result in suspecting that particular location as having been disturbed. Neither dogs, metal detectors, nor any other type of known detection devices would help in disclosing this location.

He had no intention of digging up his treasure in the near future. No attempt would be made until he was confident the FBI had finally relented and placed his investigation toward the bottom of the heap of cases demanding their theretofore neglected attention. Regardless if that point in time arrived within weeks or even months, Sam felt he had prepared himself to adequately survive, albeit it in a far less lavish lifestyle than the more opulent one he ultimately planned to bask in.

Even with his modest salary, he had been responsible for supporting no one but himself. That had permitted him over the past couple of years to establish a savings account that would allow him to meet his monthly expenses with just a little more assistance from an outside source of income. That included four different credit card accounts with zero balances owed and the ability to borrow over 75 thousand dollars while making only the minimum monthly payments. He didn't plan to get himself into a financial bind like that, but it was at least a viable option if his miserly existence dragged on too long.

One of the most risky and initial elements of Sam's plan was leaving the armored car at the airport while still being able to claim he had been picked up by an unidentified truck driver who dropped him off near the police department following the robbery. Weeks earlier, he had found a spot far from the terminal seldom used by air travelers or employees to park their vehicles. He made sure there was no evidence of surveillance cameras that could identify activity at that location.

Not far from the spot was a recreational walking/bicycle trail that wound its way back up near the city center. In the back of the armored car, Sam had discretely stored a used bike he had previously purchased with cash from a garage sale in a minority neighborhood in Las Vegas. After parking the armored car at the selected spot in the airport parking lot and somewhat disguising his appearance with a large brimmed hat and a face mask sometimes used by pollution sufferers, both of which were subsequently discarded in an untraceable trash can, he transferred the bike to the trail and proceeded on his merry way.

Luckily, he didn't think anyone saw him exit the armored car with the bike or notice him park it in the bike rack at the local elementary school where he walked the rest of the way to the police station after discretely disposing of the hat and mask. As it turned out, there was never a witness who came forth to place him exiting the armored car or riding the bike into the city. This high-risk part of his plan had turned out to be no problem at all. He never picked up the bike from the rack with little chance it would ever expose his use of it to carry out his scheme. It would most likely end up being stolen since he hadn't locked it. What irony.

It only took the police a little less than an hour to discover the armored car at the airport. The sole recovery consisted of the coins. The only potential evidence they discovered included the fingerprints of Sam and a couple of the other drivers. Sam's description of the robbers wearing gloves conveniently explained why their alleged presence couldn't be verified. The fact no incriminating strange hairs or fibers could be found didn't prove anything in attempting to discredit Sam's signed statement.

Sam had planted some potential evidence at the scene on the dirt road where he said the robbers dropped him off. Previously, while up in Salt Lake City, he had purchased with cash two pairs of different sized used gym shoes from a local thrift store. He also disguised his identity to a somewhat lesser degree than when buying the barrels in Las Vegas. He created shoe prints at the crime scene, careful to make sure the prints logically indicated the two Hispanics entering and exiting the armored car. The shoes were thrown in the same hole as the cash.

The FBI eventually recovered the prints with a plaster of Paris kit before the rains subsequently washed them away. Sam considered that a stroke of genius on his part since those prints could later be referred to as supporting his claim of innocence. He wouldn't let himself become overconfident, but he was self-assured enough to believe his ingenuity would ultimately prevail.

FIVE

Sam's boss, Ralph, drove down from Salt Lake City to meet with him at the UNI office in St. George the day after the robbery. The confrontation went just about exactly as Sam thought it would with one additional bonus he hadn't anticipated.

"I'm sorry Sam but there's simply no way I can keep you on the payroll if you're unwilling to take a polygraph examination to help prove your innocence. It's not I don't believe you. I do. It's just its company policy. You know that. And now, to make matters worse, you're telling me you can't answer any more questions. I appreciate the copy of the statement you gave to the FBI, but you're expected to answer any additional questions I might have and your refusal to do so leaves me no alternative."

"Look boss, I understand all of that, but I have no illusion of being able to go back to work with UNI. I don't expect you to understand where I'm coming from, but I was scared to death and thought I was going to be murdered. To be absolutely honest, I'm not sure I could return to work even if you were willing to give me the chance. I would love to answer your questions, but an attorney I trust has told me to keep my mouth shut and not to talk to anyone else about the robbery. I can't believe anybody would think I may have been involved, but he says I should go forward under that assumption."

"Ok, if you're sure that's the way you want to play it. I think you're making a big mistake, but it's your decision. Tell you what I'll be willing to do. I'll fire you with the reason being you wouldn't take the polygraph but your refusal was based in good faith due to the advice of your attorney. That way you'll most likely be able to qualify for unemployment benefits. I have to be honest with you. If somebody calls me for a recommendation, I'm going to feel compelled to tell them about your refusal. That may not go over too well."

"I can appreciate your position," Sam dutifully responded. "Thanks for giving me that much of a break. I want you to know I'm totally innocent. I only hope that one day soon they are able to capture the two who have ruined my career and potentially the chance of ever getting another job of any worth. Mostly, I hope then you will know for an absolute certainty I was telling the truth."

He hadn't anticipated the extra bonus of unemployment checks to help tide him over until he could get his hands on the loot. This meant he may not have to depend that much on borrowing against his credit cards after all.

On the way to the office that morning, he hadn't noticed the surveillance plane circling high overhead or the three nondescript trail vehicles that had traded places as they followed him to the office and back home. He didn't need to know for sure if he was being tailed. He assumed he was. He expected it to happen. He would have been totally shocked if it wasn't taking place now and for a reasonable period to come. Part of his master plan anticipated it.

That plan postulated any failed FBI strategies that took time and effort would help discourage further investigative efforts and hasten the time when Sam could start benefitting from his stash. It was based on that assumption he made a trip later in the afternoon following the interview with his boss to a storage facility located about 40 miles north in Cedar City, Utah. He rented a small shed, provided a false name/ address and pre-paid in cash for the next three months.

Luckily, the attendant didn't ask to see proof of his identity. If he had, Sam would have said he left his wallet in the car and never returned. He would have then proceeded to a number of other similar facilities to try again until he could get away with not having to prove who he was. He was counting on the use of cash to prevent that from happening. It worked out better than he could have hoped. The first attempt was the charm.

"FBI! I need to talk to you about someone who left your facility about an hour ago." It had taken SA Cook about that long to travel to Cedar City after getting the call from the team leader on the surveillance. The young attendant said there had only been one person who had come in during that period of time and he matched exactly the description of Sam including the bright orange jacket the team had noted as part of the initial entries in their log.

Reading from the agreement signed by Sam, the attendant related, "He said his name was Don Roberts and he was in the process of moving here from California. He said he hadn't found a place in Cedar City yet, but he gave his former address in San Diego. He said he was downsizing and would undoubtedly have some things he would have to temporarily place in storage."

SA Cook instructed, "I'm going to need the original of that agreement. Don't touch it anymore. I'm going to put it in this plastic protector. You can make a copy of it." Careful not to include his fingerprints on the document, Cook carefully placed the agreement in the plastic sleeve. "Did he put anything into the storage shed?"

"No, he said he would be coming back sometime in the next few days."

"Can I trust you not to let him know about our meeting today? It's extremely important this person, who by the way has given you a false name, not know that the FBI has been looking into his affairs. Can you contact me at this phone number at my office in

St. George the next time he shows up?" Cook provided a copy of his business card.

"Sure, I have no problem with that. Mum's the word. I've got my money. That's all I care about. You're not going to have a shoot-out or anything dangerous like that?"

"Absolutely not," responded Cook. "It's not that type of case. Don't worry about anything like that happening. Don't do anything out of the normal. But, it would help if you can identify any of items he ends up placing in the shed. It's not that big of shed, so it shouldn't be too much stuff."

Perfect! Just what Sam hoped would be happening.

SIX

It was early Monday morning, slightly more than a week after the robbery. SAs Hilton and Cook were sitting across the desk from Assistant United States Attorney (AUSA) Brent Samuelson who operated out of Salt Lake City in a satellite office in St. George less than a block from the FBI RA. Hilton and Cook had become close friends of Samuelson since most of their investigative prosecutions went through him in addition to obtaining authority for a variety of investigative techniques including search warrants.

SA Hilton got down to the purpose of the meeting. "We need you to authorize a search warrant as soon as possible to search Donahue's car, residence and a storage locker in Cedar City." AUSA Samuelson had already been briefed on the robbery and the activities of the surveillance squad up to this point in time.

"What's your probable cause to justify the warrant? You know our judges are sticklers on justifying any kind of a warrant. They always seem to lean in favor of the privacy rights of the person being targeted by the big bad government. They're usually reluctant to sign off unless our probable cause is solid."

"I don't think that's going to be a problem this time, Brent. Our boys have got him carrying five small cardboard boxes out of his house and putting them into the trunk of his car yesterday just after noon. They then have him transferring the boxes directly from his house to the storage shed he rented last week, a day after the robbery. Both the attendant and the surveillance team have him placing the boxes into the shed."

"You're going to need more than that," Samuelson interrupted.

"We know that," Dave responded. "Let me finish. I think you're going to like this next part. The attendant can absolutely verify that Donahue used a false name and address to rent the shed. That should give enough PC to search the house, his car and the shed, don't you think? Even Judge Bennet would be hard pressed to argue with that."

"I agree. Let's get it done. Help me draft the proposed warrant and I'll get it over to the judge this afternoon. You should be able to proceed with the search by late afternoon. Do all three locations simultaneously so he isn't able to destroy any evidence. I'll make it so you can search anything you want. That's because the stolen bills are small enough they could be hidden anywhere, but make sure to leave everything like you found it. We don't want to be accused later of destroying any of his property. That just gives the defense a chance to muddle the issue."

"Don't worry about any of that," SA Hilton assuredly responded. "I'll be in charge of the overall search. We'll use some of the guys down from Salt Lake to make sure Donahue can't get rid of evidence once we start. It's not the first time I've executed a warrant. I know what I'm doing."

"Do me one more favor, Dave. See if he will agree to a consent search before you execute the warrant. I don't expect him to, but it would simplify things if he would. Have him sign one of your consent waivers if he agrees."

"No problem, but don't count on it. From the way he clammed up after furnishing his initial signed statement, I don't think he is going to consent to anything. Now, a couple of more matters for future consideration: Can you get a couple of subpoenas for his bank and phone records? Maybe we can even start thinking about a phone tap."

"The subpoenas are a given. I'll have my secretary prepare those by day's end. The tap is problematic. Unless, you can get someone who can testify they've talked to Donahue on the phone we intend to tap concerning something incriminating about the robbery, we'll never be able to authorize it. The Department of Justice in Washington has to authorize taps on cases like this and they are very demanding on what it takes to get approval. It isn't as easy as when you can show a connection to a crime like terrorism which we obviously can't."

Later that afternoon, it was just as SA Hilton had predicted. He approached Donahue in his driveway just as he was returning from a trip to the grocery store. Donahue apologized, but said he was unwilling to voluntarily consent to a search. He accepted a copy of the warrant and allowed the agents entry to begin the search of his home. He also provided his car keys to begin the search there. He refused to answer any other questions. The concurrent search of the shed in Cedar City was also set into motion by a call from Hilton to Cook who was on the scene there.

Over four hours later, an exhaustive search of the house and car turned up nothing of an incriminating nature. No hidden compartments, suspicious cash currency, questionable bank records, shady packing materials, compromising shopping receipts. Nothing, nada, zip! Both the house and the car were cleaner than a bar of unopened soap as far as contributing to any kind of evidence that might criminally implicate Donahue. Pictures were taken of the disguise materials found in the apartment but the items weren't confiscated because they couldn't be logically tied in any way to the suspected theft. The search was a bust to say the least.

As for the shed, the four cardboard boxes contained nothing but used books. It soon became readily apparent Donahue had been purposely misleading the FBI. Although he wasn't about to admit to it, the pompous prick (SA Cook's description) was deliberately toying with the investigation of him. There could be little doubt now he was guilty, but he was so overconfident about not being caught he was rubbing it in. Unfortunately, trying to charge him with some minor misdemeanor count of furnishing false information to the shed owner would amount to nothing of consequence if anything at all.

The news of the failed search was severely disconcerting to the members of the Salt Lake City surveillance team. It was now apparent the suspect was well aware he was being followed everywhere he went. The chances of catching him doing something inculpating were now mostly negligible. They would complete their agreement for the remainder of the week, but there were more promising fish to pursue on other high priority cases back at headquarters.

SEVEN

There could be no doubt a primary motive for Sam's misappropriation was the more opulent lifestyle he would realize once he was able to utilize his ill-gotten gain. But, there was another motivating rationality that had driven him as well. Up until he started contriving his scheme, his life had degenerated into a downward spiral of a monotonous work ethic interspersed with somewhat boring and depressing periods in-between.

The months of careful contriving had provided him with a sense of exhilaration causing him to anticipate each new day as another opportunity to create the perfect crime. Life had new meaning. He enthusiastically used his spare time to think and rethink every element of what it would take to be successful. He was actually enjoying his life like never before. Every day presented a new and exciting challenge in creating a perfect plan of attack.

After initiating his plan to the point of no return, he had even started a scrapbook to record his accomplishments. The first page consisted of a newspaper clipping recounting the alleged robbery. Next, a copy of his signed statement. The third and fourth pages included copies of his storage shed rental and the receipt of the search warrant that confirmed nothing incriminating had been taken during the search of his house, car and shed.

Although a rationale for the ruse with the shed was to attempt to hasten the end of a concentrated surveillance of his movements, Sam could have eliminated that element of his master plan and therefore not unduly incensed the FBI. That may have been the more prudent direction to pursue. However, it wouldn't have been half the fun. He enjoyed matching wits with America's finest. It made the heist that much more gratifying.

Back in their office, The SAs were rapidly approaching the initial stages of exasperating agitation.

"Who does this guy think he is, anyway?" Cook lamented. "Is he crazy? I'm sure he has to realize the deal with the shed just makes him look guiltier. If we had any lingering doubts before, that cinches him as the sole viable suspect. What kind of game is he playing?"

"He obviously doesn't care if he makes himself look guiltier," Hilton countered. "He apparently wants us to know he did it and there isn't going to be anyway we can prove it. We're going to have to prove him wrong. Egotists like him always make one or more unsurmountable mistakes. They think they're perfect but they're not. My guess is he's already slipped up in some way he doesn't know about or he's going to slip up in the future. It's up to us to figure out how. By the way, how did your interviews with his fellow employees go?"

"Not so good. They all say he's one honest dude and they can't imagine him in their wildest dreams ever being part of a crime. They claim he's never said anything to any of them indicating he would consider stealing any money. To the man, they're certain he was robbed as he claimed. They think he got a raw deal by being terminated. Nothing there at all that's going to assist us in making the case against him. How did you do with the neighbors?"

"About the same depressing results. Nothing that's going to help us so far. The truth is none of them know him very well or have any opinion one way or the other as to his possible guilt or innocence. He evidently hasn't interacted very much with any of them. Kind of a lone wolf. I've got a couple of them who have agreed to contact us if they observe anything suspicious, but I'm not putting much stock in being able to get positive results from what I anticipate will be their less than enthusiastic assistance."

"What about a reward?" Cook questioned. "That might make a difference, don't you think?"

"I have no doubt there's going to be a substantial reward we're going to be able to use to our benefit. I'm thinking maybe as much as $50,000 or even more. The insurance companies will most likely pony up that much. I wouldn't be surprised if the Bureau kicked in some too. Of course, that only has the potential for success if one or more witnesses actually know something about Donahue's guilt. One problem we'll encounter for sure will be a slew of calls with all kinds of phony claims while accomplishing nothing but to divert our time and attention from where we need to be directing it."

"You're probably right," Cook lamented, "but maybe a decent reward might, at least, get the neighbors to be a little more attentive."

Donahue hadn't disregarded the possibility of rewards or other incentives to make a case against him. That's why he would have never considered the theft if he wasn't confident no one and that meant absolutely no one would be aware before and after the fact of any of the evidentiary details that could land him in the slammer.

He had seen and heard enough to know that low life opportunists would commit perjury to benefit themselves in one way or another. Fellow prisoners were notorious for falsely ratting out their cell mates to lessen their own exposure. Sam hopefully didn't have to worry about being jailed, but anybody could make up anything about him to qualify for a reward or benefit in some other fashion.

Rewards, however, were normally contingent on being paid only when the lead resulted in the successful prosecution of the target. Before a top-notch prosecutor would rely on the testimony of an alleged witness, the past credibility and possible motivations of the witness would be carefully scrutinized. Such witnesses were often subjected to a polygraph exam if there was any question.

Sam figured the extremely slight possibility of law enforcement coming up with one or more phony witnesses who could successfully accuse him of guilt was well worth the risk. Any proficient defense attorney simply wouldn't allow testimony like that to prevail even if some desperate prosecutor endeavored to go that route.

EIGHT

Sam wasn't dumb. As a teenager, his father had hired a psychologist to give him an IQ test. He thought his son seemed brighter than his friends and was curious to find out just how much more intelligent he might be. Sam scored a 126 which indicated a "very superior intelligence" and the likely probability of successfully progressing to post graduate study.

The problem was Sam's grades in high school didn't match his recorded intelligence. He flunked several classes and spent two summers making them up. He barely was able to graduate high school. Trying to look back on it now with an open mind, he attributed boredom, poor teachers and a corresponding bad attitude to his less than sterling academic performance. He figured now he might have graduated at the top of his class under different circumstances.

He rationalized there were primarily two main reasons he had never made a serious attempt to attend college or better himself through some other form of structured training. First, his early marriage had forced him to take both full and part-time jobs to make ends meet. The best his 18 year old wife could do was working 20 hours/week at minimum wage. For the first few years, that left little opportunity for considering any kind of higher education.

That didn't explain why he hadn't gone back to school later when his economic situation improved. He had to admit now the second reason superseded the first one. He simply had no patience for teachers who he considered less intelligent than himself. The thought of sitting through endless classes with perceived dimwits was more than he could fathom. He realized now that kind of superior attitude had probably been a big mistake. He had seriously considered going back to school to improve his lot in life, but in the end had decided that perpetrating the perfect crime offered the most potential fulfillment.

He seemed to have a special gift for memory retention. When he put his mind to it, he could quickly memorize almost anything. A few years ago he had checked out a book from the local library by memory expert Harry Lorayne entitled, *How to develop a SUPER-POWER MEMORY*. Basically, the book taught associating difficult to recall words and numbers with objects that had meaning. Linking objects together by imagining logical fantasies for the connections then allowed a person to connect lengthy lists of topics and numbers.

One of the parlor tricks taught by Lorayne was to take a deck of cards and have a person turn the cards over one at a time. After all the cards were turned face down, Sam would have the person provide a number between 1 and 52. After counting down into the pile that number, he could easily tell the person which card it was before turning it over. The trick was to associate and link. Sam found he could not only use the system to successfully perform the apparent magic, but he also seemed to have the uncanny ability to remember the location of many of the cards without depending on the need to associate and link. This confirmed what he had suspected for some time now. He had apparently been gifted with something approaching a photographic memory.

Eventually, he decided to use his newfound skill at the blackjack tables in Nevada. He determined he could remember an amazing number of the cards played. Instead of the house maintaining the advantage, he found himself gaining an edge. The problem was he didn't have enough of a stake to make his unique talent payoff in a meaningful way. Still, he enjoyed the atmosphere of the casino and could play a long time while routinely winning more times than losing.

Sam, the suddenly skilled card shark, subsequently got his hands on a self-published pamphlet by a former Las Vegas blackjack dealer who explained a couple more strategies to help beat the odds. First, the player should never double down or split pairs. Doing so gave the advantage to the house.

Second, betting should proceed in a specific manner. The pamphlet provided a chart based on the initial bankroll of the player, how to bet on no more than 4 consecutive rounds, and when to quit based on how much winnings had been accumulated. For example, with a bankroll of $300, the player should quit after winning $100. A maximum of 4 rounds should proceed with progressive bets of $5, 4X ($20), 5X ($25), and 10X ($50).

Depending on the starting bankroll, the initial bet varied but the multiple progressions of the next three bets remained the same. For example, for a $6,000 bankroll, the initial bet was $100 followed by $400, $500, and $1000. Betting would then be discontinued when winnings reached $2000.

Finally, to hone his skills even more, Sam decided to incorporate one of several systems known as card counting. These systems were grounded on the theory that with a higher percentage of larger cards still not dealt by the dealer, the player had the advantage that (1) the dealer would bust more often, (2) the player would be dealt more blackjacks and (3) the player would be dealt stronger and higher starting hands.

All the systems started the count at 0. For the system chosen by Sam, 1 was added to cards #s 2-6 and 1 was subtracted for 10, J, Q, K and A. Nothing was added or subtracted for #s 7-9. Obviously, the higher the count prior to any bet, the better chance for the player to realize success.

The problem was that casinos reserved the right to exclude anyone from betting on their tables. If they, for example, concluded a player was counting cards, they routinely barred such players from their establishment. Cameras were focused on every blackjack table and expert watchers were adept at spotting card counters. That reality was another reason he had purchased numerous disguises at the Hollywood specialty store. That was the justification he would provide should the disguises identified in the search warrant of his residence ever come up in any future attempt to tie them to the theft. After all, card counting wasn't a crime.

By using a combination of his innate gift of memory and his mastery of the card playing strategies, he concluded his talent at the blackjack table would provide a significant element leading to the ultimate success of his master plan.

NINE

It had now been a little over two weeks since SAs Hilton and Cook had begun their investigation of what they now privately referred to as the Sam Scam. The probe was centered on Donahue and nobody else. They weren't concerned some future defense attorney for him might chastise the FBI for failing to consider even the slightest possibility their client might have been telling the truth in his initial signed statement. His ploy with the storage shed had convinced them he had stolen the cash and was flaunting his perceived invulnerability in their faces.

"He's playing with us and wasting our time," Cook lamented as he reported the results of his early morning surveillance. "I followed him for over two hours. He led me on a wild goose chase back up I-15 to Cedar City and drove past the same storage shed. It was like he was rubbing it in. I don't think he made my tail but who knows for sure. Then he went up over Cedar Mountain and pulled off onto a dirt road. I hid my car and observed him getting out of his and walking up into the trees. He was carrying a trash bag full of something and returned empty handed."

"I'm guessing from your demeanor this wasn't the break we've been hoping for," Dave lamented.

"You got that right. He retraced his tracks once again driving past the shed and returning back to his apartment. After I radioed you to sit on his apartment in case he took off again, I went back to the spot where he got out of the car and easily found the buried bag. It was filled with this." Cook spilled the contents of the bag on Hilton's desk that included bundles of play money wrapped in rubber bands.

"Asshole," Hilton reacted. "He obviously thinks he has us over a barrel. Right now, he considers himself invulnerable and it's that arrogance that's going to prove to be his downfall. The two of us may not be able to follow him everywhere for much longer, but he's eventually going to have to retrieve the cash and attempt to spend it. It's not going to do him any good to leave it wherever it's being hidden. The money's going to have to show up eventually and we'll have all our bases covered when it does."

"I hope you're right." Steve still wasn't as confident as his senior partner, but he agreed their only viable option was to prepare the best they could to catch Donahue when the money started to surface. That included keeping a close watch over his spending, constantly reviewing his bank account and money-related records, and making sure any significant asset purchases could be justified within the parameters of his legitimate sources of income.

"One piece of good news," Dave added. "I just got off the phone with Salt Lake and they have agreed to loan us the full surveillance unit again next week. This time they'll stick around for at least two more weeks. I convinced them Donahue may become over confident if he thinks we're the only two following him and we're starting to let up in desperation. So, over the next few days, we need to make sure to reinforce that impression"

"Now, for some not so good news," Dave continued. "The AUSA has declined to allow us to sneak a beeper onto his car to make it easier for us to follow from a distance. He said we didn't have enough probable cause for the judge to sign off. I figured that might happen. The only stuff we have is evidence of his taunting crap and that evidently isn't going to cut it. Unless we come up with some more concrete evidence tied directly to the theft, the chance of getting anymore search warrants has diminished, at least for now."

"I guess that means tapping his phone is still out of the question." Steve sarcastically reacted.

"No kidding, Sherlock! Like AUSA Samuelson already told us, something like that takes way more probable cause and requires Justice Department approval in Washington. Until we're able to round up a reliable witness who can testify to a recent conversation over the phone in question about something relating directly to Donahue's guilt, that remains a no-go. Of course, we've already been able to subpoena his phone records to determine the identity of who he's talking to, but that avenue has so far proved fruitless. His use of the phone has been limited to say the least. It makes you wonder if he has any friends let alone any confederates in crime."

"Same thing with his bank records," Steve lamented. "So far, at least, the only deposit to this point has been his final check from UNI. His unemployment checks will most likely be showing up in the near future. His only withdrawals to date consist of cash from the ATM. He hasn't used credit or debit cards as far as I've been able to determine. I don't think he's going to be stupid enough to run any of the stolen money through the only bank account I've been able to identify."

"You're probably right," Dave agreed. "What we'll do, of course, is conduct a continuing net worth investigation on his financial activities. At the point we can show he's spending more than his legitimate income allows, that will allow the kind of probable cause we need to get things moving on the fast track. So once again, until he finally decides to start utilizing some of the loot, it may be difficult to make much headway."

The problem with the investigative prowess of both SAs was that Sam wasn't about to take any unnecessary chances by allowing their fact-finding techniques to prevail. He had already decided he wouldn't get anywhere near the money for most likely several months after the robbery. Even then, he was prepared to go much longer until he was absolutely sure he wasn't being followed. Until then, he might play a few more of his games to keep life interesting and discourage their surveillance of him. All his planning had been concocted well in advance of the theft. He had tried his best to anticipate all moves by the FBI, insurance investigators and anyone else who might try to expose him.

Sam Donahue was no dope and justifiably confident the perfect crime was well within his grasp.

TEN

One of the main reasons for the lack of possible informants to help the FBI keep track of any suspicious activity on the part of Donahue had to do with his religious belief or more to the point his lack thereof. He was an Agnostic in a sea of Mormons. That included the vast majority of his neighbors and former work associates.

Social and civic activities in St. George most often centered on the Mormon Church. Members didn't purposely exclude those who didn't share in their faith, but neither did they go out of their way to socialize with them. Most non-members did eventually get a visit from the full-time missionaries with an invitation to learn more about the denomination and join them in Sunday services. Sam made it clear he wasn't interested and had doubts about organized religion in general. That refusal ended up with him living a somewhat isolated local life outside of work.

It wasn't that he was ignorant about the dogma of Christianity or most major religions for that matter. There had been a time earlier in his life when he had studiously looked into such beliefs. He once read and seriously pondered the Bible from beginning to end. He did the same for other sacred books including the Koran. He had concluded all these various scriptures were most likely the creation of humans and had nothing to do with input from any of the claimed super-natural beings.

That didn't mean there wasn't some godly entity out there somewhere who had something to do with the creation of earth and the human race. It was just that Sam hadn't found any convincing evidence in any organized religion to prove such divinity existed. So, until he ran across more convincing validation, he would remain a committed Agnostic asserting there was no way at present to know for sure one way or the other. What he was sure of was no existing religious group including the Mormons appeared to have a persuasive clue.

One of the most common religious tenets causing him to distrust organized religion was the belief in a final judgment where humans were assigned to Heaven or Hell based on a test of how well they had lived their lives in mortality. That made no sense to Sam because there was no uniform test that could be applied fairly to everyone who has or will eventually have inhabited earth. What about infants who died before they could be tested? Did they just go directly to Heaven? How fair was that if they might have slipped up had they grown up to be tested? That seemed like an almost unfair advantage of dying young. Yet, certainly, they wouldn't deserve being sent to Hell.

How about comparing someone who grew up in a ghetto with someone who grew up in an atmosphere far more conducive to leading a successful and moral life? How could any god know for sure if those persons from the exceptional lifestyles wouldn't have gone down the wrong path had they been subjected to a poor environment? What about the other way around?

If there was one true church and one true god who dictated the commandments that had to be followed to be saved, what about the vast majority of those who never had an opportunity to learn about those particular saving commandments? How could they be fairly judged when comparing them to those who had the advantage of knowing what they had to do to achieve celestial status?

Sam figured the only way a test had any value would be if everyone taking the test had an equal opportunity to succeed or fail. Mortality simply didn't offer that. That meant the idea of a final judgment was bogus. If the primary idea of organized religion was to judge humans on how well they followed any number of conflicting and/or unknown commandments, the concept of any fairly administered test was totally ludicrous.

The supposed God of the Bible was equally incomprehensible. How could the God of the Old Testament possibly be construed as having anything to do with Jesus of the New Testament? One was mean and vindictive while the other appeared to be kind and gentle. Sam had long ago concluded Jesus Christ was more likely no more than one in a string of human Jewish prophets. It was more likely the deluded Paul who had deviously marketed him into a Christian God.

Sam was adamant a person could be just as moral being an Agnostic as a devoted member of an organized religion. That was mainly because he was convinced it was mere humans who had concocted the supposed revelations from their alleged gods. That meant all organized religious morals were nothing more than humanly devised. It was mortals, not gods, who therefore had not only the capacity but had in fact created their own long list of moral imperatives.

Anyway, the end result was that he didn't have many dealings with the Mormons. Crimes are often solved with associates, both close and not so close, who have regular contact with the suspect and engage in numerous conversations, any one of which may provide evidence of wrongdoing. Close associates are also more likely to know when the lifestyle of a suspect has taken a suspicious turn out of the ordinary. Contacting anyone with that type of connection was highly unlikely as far as Sam and St. George were concerned.

Some might conclude he would have been less likely to go through with his unlawful scheme had he been a devout Christian faced with certain punishment in the hereafter. After all, one of the Ten Commandments made it clear stealing of that magnitude would most likely be subject to dire eternal consequences even if the thief got away with it on earth. That might appear like a logical speculation, but the truth was he had never once considered being an Agnostic as a rationale to risk the theft.

He had always calculated that going to prison was sufficiently horrific enough in its own right to make him think twice before transgressing the law. Religion appeared to allow for the saving grace of repentance that could limit the degree of eternal punishment. So, even if he had been religiously inclined, it would have been the worldly justice system, not the spiritual one, that would have acted as a deterrent to committing a crime.

The thought of spending a significant amount of time in prison was reason enough to frighten him. He couldn't think of anything worse than having his freedom and privacy taken away for a prolonged period of time. That's why he had spent so much time and effort in making sure that wouldn't happen. That's the reason he would have never gone through with the theft unless he had been absolutely sure there was essentially no chance of ever being incarcerated.

ELEVEN

"Hey partner, do you realize it's almost midnight? You woke me up! What's going on?" SA Cook was slightly irritated but more curious as to why his senior partner was calling him this late. This was the first time he had been called that late by Dave during their brief six months together. He was considerate that way. It must be something important.

"Sorry to get you up buddy, but I just got woken too and we both need to hustle over to the office. The Salt Lake team called me a few minutes ago to let us know Donahue is moving. Who knows what that means? It's highly unusual, though. He's never left the house this late before. They have him headed north on highway 18 toward the Dixie National Forest. They want us to standby in case they need us for a search or possible arrest depending on where he goes and what he does."

"No problem, I'll be over there in about fifteen. Maybe this is the night we finally catch a break."

"Big Bird to Alpha 1. Hit your break lights so I can tell which car you're in."-- "Thanks, I figured that was you. Not many cars on 18 this time of night. That's the target a couple of hundred yards ahead of you." The surveillance plane was up and in place to follow Donahue wherever he might be headed. "I'm assuming the three cars following you are part of us."

"That's 10-4 on both counts. Alphas 2, 3 and 4 are behind me. Should be fairly easy from this point on. The only risk is for any of us getting too close since we're about the only ones out tonight. That's why we're counting on you to let us know what's going on up ahead."

"Shouldn't be a problem Alpha 1. He's got distinctive tail lights that are hard to miss."

"Sounds good, Big Bird. The way I have it figured he should be approaching the town of Central in the next couple of minutes."

"I can see the lights of what appears to be some kind of all-night convenience store with gas pumps outside."

"That's definitely Central. I doubt anything else would be lighted up this time of night."

"OK guys, heads up! I have the target pulling over and stopping at the convenience store. Looks like he's just sitting there. He's not getting out."

"This is Alpha 1 to all units. I'm going to drive by and keep on going. The rest of you hold back around the curve out of sight. Alpha 2 you pick up an extremely loose tail after Big Bird lets us know where the target's headed next. The rest of you stay way back out of sight. I don't want target to see your headlights."

"Alpha 2, 10-4." "Alpha 3, 10-4." "Alpha 4, 10-4." "Big Bird, 10-4."

"This is Big Bird. Target has pulled out of the station and headed north again on 18. Alpha 2, he's all yours."

"10-4, Big Bird. I can't see his tail lights yet so keep me advised."

"OK, target is turning right, that's turning east on a road about one mile north of Central. Looks like he's headed right into the thick of the Dixie Forest area."

"Alpha 2 to Big Bird. I'm turning right. Am I on the right road?"

"10-4 Alpha 2. That's the road. Might be better if you turn off your headlights if you can still follow the road. I estimate you're about 500 yards behind right now."

"Shouldn't be a problem. The moon's pretty bright tonight."

"Alpha 1 to 3 and 4. Hang back in the Central area for now and I'll stay north of where target turned off in case he comes back out and heads this way."

"This is Alpha 3. We're both at the gas station waiting for further instructions."

"All units, this is Big Bird. It appears target has turned off his lights. I can't see him anymore. The trees are too thick to see anything unless he turns his lights back on."

Sam had turned his lights off and turned off into the far corner of one of a multitude of camp sites in the Dixie National Forest Park. He then sought further cover about 100 feet beyond into the thick of the trees where he couldn't be easily observed even if someone pulled into the site to see if that's where he went. He got out of the car and in the still of the evening air could hear the faint buzz of a plane circling high overhead.

Shortly thereafter, he heard and observed the outline of a car with its lights out pass by. There was little doubt that he was being followed; most likely, by a full and highly trained FBI surveillance team, but he didn't know for sure. What mattered was a determination the observation of his travel was continuing at a high level and it would be a while longer before he could even consider the possibility of traveling in the direction of the cash.

Not caring that he was being followed, he reversed his course and headed back to his apartment. He immediately turned his lights on so the plane could see where he had been hiding. Back in his apartment, he wondered how long they would stay in the forest trying to determine what he may have hidden or picked up.

"This is Alpha 1 calling off the search. He most likely heard the plane. There's no way he would have turned on his lights so that we could see where he had pulled off unless he's playing with us again. Since he's back at his apartment now, there's no reason to think he going anywhere else tonight. Sorry to keep you all up so late."

Dave was rapidly coming to the conclusion the Salt Lake team was wasting their valuable time. He would probably tell them tomorrow to head back to headquarters city. Dave and Steve headed back home for what little remained of a short night's siesta.

TWELVE

Over the past year, Sam had made it a practice to spend what little off time he had to gamble at selected casinos and their blackjack tables in Mesquite and Las Vegas, Nevada. He wanted to make sure he had witnesses who could confirm that he was a player capable of sustained exceptional blackjack play. His plan required it.

He wanted a few carefully selected casino employees to recognize him. The use of disguises would come later. He didn't bet much because he didn't have much to bet. His normal routine included buying $100 of chips at a blackjack table and playing with the advantage of his sterling memory and the card playing schemes he had been slowly perfecting. He realized no matter how well he played, casinos hadn't built their luxurious surroundings by allowing players to win more than they lost. Still, he was now more than confident he could do way better than the average loser.

With his scheme requiring the reputation of possessing the blackjack skills to win big, he was slowly gaining that distinction. Although he also lost from time to time, his potential witnesses remembered mostly his winning ways because he made sure to tip them generously from his proceeds. They included some cocktail waitresses in short skirts and seasoned dealers who had remained employed at the same casino over an extended period of time. He figured they would most likely still be there if he needed them later on to substantiate his potential for expert play.

Not wanting to be posted on the unwelcome list of even a single casino for being a card counter, Sam took cautionary steps to help ensure he didn't match the profile for possible exclusion. He purposely lost just enough so anyone following his play would soon lose interest because his play wasn't costing the casino anything approaching an amount that would cause a warning bell to sound. He continually had to carefully weigh both sides of a fine line that divided creating the impression of being an extraordinarily skilled player while not jeopardizing a casino's bottom line. The risk of drawing undue attention and possible ejection was constantly on his mind.

The scheming required the FBI and anyone else who was interested in proving his guilt and recovering the stolen funds to be well aware of his proclivity to regularly test his skill at blackjack. In order to solidify that impression, Sam first assured himself he was being followed and then led his shadow pursuers to the casinos where his chosen potential witnesses worked. On more than one occasion, he was actually able to spot one of the two FBI agents who had initially interviewed him skulking in the distant background of the blackjack playing area.

"Apparently, our man plays a lot of blackjack. I was able to develop a couple of sources who say he's quite skilled. Doesn't seem he gambles on much of anything else the best I could tell. One of the waitresses, who's quite stunning I might add, says he wins more than most of the customers she runs into. The thing is he's a low stakes customer and there's not much money involved when he plays. He just seems to like the atmosphere and the challenge of winning." SA Cook's report to his partner was being met with some hopeful interest.

"Can you tell if he's playing with more money than he can legitimately account for?"

"I'm afraid not," Steve responded. "At least not at this point in time. The amount of chips he purchases doesn't look to be greater than what he can account for from his legal sources of income. In checking his ATM withdrawals, it would be hard to prove those withdrawals aren't the sole source of his betting. He definitely favors the use of cash. The Visa card in his name is used only rarely."

"Regardless," Dave directed. "You need to keep on top of this. I wouldn't be surprised if he has some kind of addiction to gambling. If that's the case, it means he may be tempted in the not too distant future to take a large chunk of the stolen cash and gamble it away. We need to develop liaison with the casinos he seems to favor and keep track of how much he bets. I think we're pretty solid on his legit net worth and his use of anything above that might give us the kind of proof we need to tie this baby up in a nice little bow."

It was now well into the second month of the investigation. Dave and Steve were pretty much on their own. The Salt Lake surveillance squad was nothing more than a rapidly fading memory. They weren't about to be invited back unless there was a near certainly their services would prove fruitful. Their previous appearances on the scene had proven embarrassing to say the least. No self- respecting FBI Senior RA agent wants to gain the reputation of crying wolf too often.

To make matters even more problematic, Dave's forced retirement was now less than two months away and a reward that had now reached a total of $100,000 had yet to yield even a single clue. Replacing Dave would most likely take a few weeks and leave Steve holding down the shop by himself for up to a month. There would be little opportunity for him to concentrate on the Sam Scam and still handle the priority leads constantly streaming into the RA for immediate action. It was possible Steve could get some temporary help from Salt Lake, but he wasn't holding his breath. Everyone seemed to be preoccupied with their own compelling investigations.

RAYMOND A. HULT

Sam read an article in the local newspaper concerning the imminent retirement of SA Hilton. He wasn't about to make a move unless he was absolutely convinced he couldn't be detected. It was, however, rapidly becoming obvious the constant surveillance of his activities was on a significant downward slide. He was becoming more and more optimistic the initial phase for the retrieval of the stolen cash might commence sooner than he had originally anticipated.

THIRTEEN

The $100,000 of reward money had all been tendered by the Pingree and Golden Insurance Agency (P&G) who had previously negotiated a Cash-in-Transit coverage policy with UNI. P&G was one of the few agencies who provided such coverage to the armored car and courier industry. They were thus the responsible party to reimburse, less a substantial UNI deductible, the various banks victimized by the theft. The deductible amounting to $200,000 would in all likelihood become the responsibility of UNI after all the dust settled.

Should the stolen funds not be recovered, the possibility of getting any insurance agency to cover UNI again would be highly problematic at best. The fact UNI had allowed a single driver to transfer such a large sum by himself would undoubtedly prove disastrous for UNI and the insurance coverage required for continuing to operate. The sad fact was P&G might successfully sue UNI for the total loss less the deductible and very likely force UNI into bankruptcy.

The reason UNI might lose such a lawsuit suit had to do with the fine print in the policy requiring UNI to maintain reasonable precautions as prescribed in industry-wide standards to prevent embezzlement and robbery. Otherwise, the attorneys for P&G would claim, and with just cause, they shouldn't be responsible for the loss. One of the industry standards cautioned that armored cars should be manned by two employees minimum. Obviously, that requirement had been ignored on more than one occasion by UNI.

The unfortunate reality was UNI wasn't capable of reimbursing a whole lot more than the deductible. Assuming P&G could prevail in the suit, the insurance policy might be held to be null and void and the banks would be left holding the bag less what UNI had been able to come up with before their likely bankruptcy petition. With its few remaining assets after paying the deductible, it was hard to conceive of UNI successfully rehabilitating itself.

The banks, of course, had their own insurance policies that would cover the majority of their losses should P&G and UNI come up short. Although the outlook for P&G looked promising because of the likely success of suit against UNI, they weren't taking any chances. They wanted their own man on the scene to work with law enforcement to recover the money.

George Beckett was a former FBI agent who had taken early retirement a couple of years earlier to join up with a nationally renowned private investigative agency headquartered out of Washington DC. He was located working with two other private investigators out of a satellite office in Denver, Colorado. Beckett was selected to look into the P&G matter when he revealed he and SA Hilton had gone through new agents training together in Quantico, Virginia.

"I've been here almost two weeks now and I'm no further finding any evidence against Donahue than when I first arrived. I've followed him all around St. George and on numerous trips to Mesquite and Las Vegas, all to no avail. I've found zip to prove he stole the money. I'm reporting back the FBI investigation doesn't appear as of yet to have developed any concrete evidence to prove Donahue did it. I hope that's OK. They're pulling me off the case. P&G figures they've spent enough money on me and their approach from here on out is to leave all further investigation to law enforcement." Beckett was sharing his final unproductive report to his old FBI training class buddy.

"Well, they can't say that you didn't try. I appreciate your effort. I don't mind you reporting your overall impression our case has stalled. Even though I've let you look at the case file, keep that to yourself. We both know I might get criticized for sharing specific details of our investigation with outsiders even if they were former fellow agents. I would appreciate your circumspection. I don't need any trouble; especially, with my pending retirement so close now. I'd like to go out on top if you know what I mean."

"Come on, you know me better than that Dave," George responded. "I've had enough personal experience in the Bureau to know how to work my final report without getting you in any kind of trouble at all. I really do appreciate your help even if you haven't yet been able to nail the perp. I can't believe he's not going to expose himself somehow when he finally starts to dig into his ill-gotten gain."

"It's been great working with you again, George. Maybe we'll cross trails again after I retire. It sounds like you struck gold with your retirement job. I haven't decided what I'm going to do yet. To be honest, I'm kind of worn out and just might retire altogether. The wife and I like to travel and it would be nice to be able to do that anytime we wanted. I think we would have enough funds to pull it off without any further employment. But, I don't know for sure yet. I'm going to think about it for a while."

Sam didn't feel all that guilty if UNI dissolved into bankruptcy and ceased to exist as a viable entity. He had warned his superiors more times than he could remember he needed more help and it was unwise to allow him to transfer money on his own. They deserved whatever fate awaited them. His fellow employees would get work with the next company to take UNI's place. The money of the banks had to be transferred and somebody was going to have to do it. Sam was much more concerned about his own neck than the necks of his former tight-fisted superiors.

As far as the private dick was concerned, it had taken no time at all to discover he was tracking Sam's movements. He played all those who were following him the same. The only information they had been able to discover was exactly what he wanted.

FOURTEEN

It had been a little over a month since the retirement of SA Hilton. The reigns for the supervision of the RA had apparently been turned over to SA Cook. From what Sam could tell, a second agent had not as yet been assigned to bring the RA back to its full complement of two full-time crime fighters.

Sam had developed a routine to help determine if he was being tailed. He continually checked for any kind of transmitter that may have been attached to his car bumper or some other hidden location. He kept his car locked in his apartment garage to make it more difficult to secretly attach such a device. He had never found one and was confident yet ever vigilant he could detect such an attachment should someone try to install it.

A plane was the most foolproof way to follow someone. But, that was mostly because the target of the surveillance didn't suspect the plane circling high above. With some diligence, the faint hum of the engine could be detected and with careful observation could even be spotted during daylight hours. No plane had been observed for well over two months now.

Car surveillance was fairly easy to notice when only one or two follow vehicles were involved. He had become expert in being able to determine if he was being tailed in that manner. All it took was to concentrate on his rear view mirror while making numerous turns and stops to fairly easily determine if the same one or two vehicles were constantly behind him. It's hard for someone to follow somebody else unless they stay close behind. If they get several cars behind, the following car will be left behind by a stoplight or some other similar hindrance. If they stay too close, on the other hand, it's easy for the person being pursued to detect.

He was confident no one had been following him for several weeks now. That included SA Cook and the third man who had followed him for a little over two weeks about a month ago. It was time to initiate the next and potentially most risky part of his master plan. If someone followed him to where he had buried the money, it would most likely prove disastrous to his entire scheme.

Returning to the burial site too often would severely increase his chances of being caught. He decided that two more trips to the site were all he could afford to make. Each trip would entail retrieving approximately half or three drums of the money. He decided on a space of several months between the two trips to completely relocate the loot.

He needed to transfer the drums to a safer location that could more easily be accessed with little chance of being discovered. Toward that end, he had rented an apartment and storage shed more than a month before the theft. He had realistically disguised his appearance so no one could identify his true identity in any kind of future lineup.

Several weeks before the rentals, Sam had flown to Albuquerque where he negotiated the purchase of a small Toyota after seeing a for sale sign in the window where the car was parked in a low rent district just within the city limits. The car was in fairly good shape even though it was 11 years old with considerable mileage. It could easily pass for being much newer. The owner was thrilled to receive his asking price of $3000 in cash. Sam planned to temporarily store the car in the long term parking lot at the airport in Las Vegas.

Licensing the car in New Mexico in his own name, he realized the chance law enforcement might discover his purchase. That, however, seemed like a remote possibility as it was hard to imagine the FBI in St. George deciding to take that step. They had no reason to suspect he had access to any vehicle other than the one he had registered in Utah. In reality, any such discovery wouldn't prove anything anyway. Tying the robbery to the purchase of a vehicle in New Mexico might appear circumstantially suspicious but far from providing solid evidence of the crime.

Sam in disguise mode had rented a reasonably priced furnished apartment in an out-of-the-way location several miles from the downtown strip in Las Vegas. He made sure the apartment included parking spaces in the rear so his car couldn't be seen from the street. He was able to pay the landlord up-front with cash and a phony name with no questions asked. It was obvious the fictitious rental form he filled out would never be checked as long as he continued to pay his rent in advance. It was apparent the landlord, who lived several blocks from the apartment, couldn't have cared less about verifying any of the application information. That was a definite plus.

He arranged to pay the rent in advance each month by mailing the landlord a cashier's check which he planned to purchase for cash at any number of banks around Las Vegas. The landlord didn't seem to consider that as suspicious in anyway. Kind of like, "what happens in Las Vegas stays in Las Vegas." Sam's only concern was the payments not be late thus causing any further inquiry.

He casually informed the landlord he was a recreational gambler from New Mexico who sporadically flew into Las Vegas and decided to rent a temporary stopover. He made sure the landlord observed his black Toyota Corolla with New Mexico plates and that the car may remain parked in the same spot for weeks on end. He also said it wouldn't be unusual for some of his friends to use of the apartment without him being present and even on rare occasions borrow his car.

The storage shed he rented was located at an isolated location in North Las Vegas that would easily enable Sam to notice someone following him before he got close. It was open twenty four-seven and it was rare for anyone else to be there; especially, late at night.

He used a false name in the same way he had gained access to the Cedar City shed. He incorporated yet another unique disguise and was able to pay cash in advance with no identification required. Sam casually indicated to the storage manager he was in the process of moving from New Mexico and he required the shed to temporarily store certain items during a process that may take several months or even longer.

The biggest danger of storing the money in a shed was that someone might break in and steal the cash. To help minimize that potential hazard, he purchased for cash an old broken down desk and two similarly dilapidated file cabinets from garage sales after which he created false compartments in each that could easily accommodate the stolen bills. It was highly unlikely anyone observing the furniture would think twice about stealing such unappealing and cumbersome to move junk. An added bonus was the shed manager wouldn't suspect a thing should the shed's contents be inspected for any reason.

So it was late September, almost five months to the day following the robbery, he struck out to move the first three drums containing approximately $750,000. He altered his appearance with an especially realistic disguise if he did say so himself. He was getting good at it; maybe not as good as the professionals, but only slightly inferior.

FIFTEEN

He spent the better part of an hour making sure he wasn't being followed before leaving St. George. It didn't really matter if someone saw him in his makeup. He could provide a perfectly reasonable and innocent explanation if he had to. Being seen in disguise mode might actually contribute to the success of his master plan. What did matter, in fact it was absolutely imperative, was preventing any followers from successfully tracking him to where the money was hidden. All his meticulous planning would be for naught should a catastrophic game-breaker like that ever materialize.

Sam parked in the New York New York casino parking lot toward the south end of the Las Vegas Strip. Making sure he wasn't being followed, he made his way on foot northward on the Strip where he caught a cab that took him to a location several blocks from his apartment. From there, he walked the rest of the way to where he had parked the Toyota. He felt it necessary to use the Toyota just in case the FBI had somehow been, albeit highly unlikely, successful in surreptitiously installing some kind of GPS transmitter device to his only known mode of transportation.

Heading back north on I-15 toward St. George, he pulled off twice to make sure he wasn't being followed. Finally, as confident as possible he was traveling unobserved, he exited I-15 and returned to where the money was entombed. After once again assuring himself there was no plane flying overhead and no one else traveling behind him, he hid his car so it couldn't be seen by a passerby and about a hundred yards across the road from the loot.

He continued on foot along a circuitous route to the burial site, careful to step on rock formations and low lying shrubbery to help preclude leaving his footprints. He removed the cover rocks, dug down to the drums with a shovel he would later discard, and covered the remaining three drums like before. He carefully retraced his steps three times more carrying one drum at a time and placing them in the trunk of his car. He then transferred the cash from the three drums to three medium sized cardboard packing boxes. He would later toss the empty drums in a garbage receptacle far removed from where they had been stored.

Passing no other vehicles on his return to I-15, he relaxed slightly for the first time in several hours and headed south through the gorge for Las Vegas. He figured he would have been pulled over by now if law enforcement had somehow successfully exposed his extremely cautious recovery plan.

Waiting nearby for it to get dark and for the operator of the storage shed to go off duty, he parked the Toyota next to his assigned shed. He was the only one there. He moved the boxes into the shed and secured the inside of the door so no one could unexpectedly open it from the outside while he was transferring the bills from the boxes to the hidden compartments in the desk and the file cabinets. The compartments were slightly wider than the width of the bills and offered secret and easy access that would be extremely difficult to detect by the casual observer.

He stuffed the boxes with old books and magazines he had brought along for that purpose and sealed the boxes shut to make it appear they were just a few more items to be temporarily stored. He returned the Toyota to its parking space behind his apartment. He then walked approximately a mile away to a small strip mall where he called a taxi that delivered him back to the Strip.

After playing at the black jack tables in New York New York for a couple of hours, he recovered his car from the parking lot and returned to St. George about 1am the following morning; far less apprehensive now that close to one-half of his ill-gotten gain was securely ensconced to allow it's retrieval with far less risk of discovering its criminal origin.

⁂

"I have to apologize, Steve. I can't really justify what took so long, but we've finally gotten you a second agent to hopefully lessen some of the pressure I know you've experienced since Dave's retirement. His name is Tony Lytle. This will be his first office since graduating out of Quantico last week. That's going to make you the Senior Resident Agent in Charge even though you haven't had all that much experience yourself. Do you think you can handle it?"

"I don't know boss. It's not going to be easy trying to fill Dave's shoes, but I'll do my best to try." Steve was in the Salt Lake Office for the purpose of conducting a periodic file review all agents were required to attend with the supervisor directly above them in the chain of command. Truth be known, he wasn't all that thrilled about having the responsibility of the RA foisted on his shoulders. Now he could be blamed not only for any of his own shortcomings, but he would be asked to account for the any mistakes of an inexperienced newcomer and whether he had received proper guidance from Steve.

"Dave highly recommended you, Steve. He said you were a quick learner and had the capability of being a terrific mentor for a first office agent. One thing for sure is both of you have a significant backlog of cases that are going to have to be brought up to date as soon as possible. I'll reassign as many cases to SA Lytle as I feel justifies his limited ability to handle them. Of course, I'll leave the armored car case to you. The fact we have yet to make an arrest bothers me. How do you see that case going now that you'll have more time to concentrate on it?"

"There's no doubt the driver did it, so it's just a matter on concentrating on him until he makes a mistake and provides us with the evidence we're going to need to move forward with an indictment. I'll be honest. So far, we haven't had much luck. A significant reward, extensive surveillance, attempting to find witnesses and informant development has as yet failed to result in any substantial evidence. It may be the only thing that trips him up is when he starts trying to spend the money. He can't hang on to it forever. We've got a solid watch going on all his income and spending. When the spending exceeds the legit income, I think that's when this case gets solved."

"I hope you're right Steve. The Salt Lake Division and your RA in particular are going to come off appearing embarrassingly incompetent if we can't solve this case sooner than later; especially, when we know who did it. We can't let this Donahue character get away with this for much longer. We need to recover the money before he spends it."

SIXTEEN

It was April and over seven months since the robbery. Now, the real challenge was about to commence. From the initial stages of his master plan, Sam had known he could never expect to utilize the stolen money unless he was first able to launder it and thus successfully explain his sudden wealth in a convincing manner that didn't tie back to his culpability in the theft.

Successfully washing the money involved a rather simple strategy, but the scheme was going to take a lot of time and unrelenting effort to successfully pull off. He wouldn't be surprised if it took months if not most of the year before the complete cleansing could be finalized. It was important the entire 1.5 million was laundered before the tax year ended. That would require he spend an inordinate amount of time at the blackjack tables scattered primarily throughout Nevada.

There were currently more than 500 casinos scattered across 29 states. Nevada led with over 200. Next in line was a virtual tie between Oklahoma and California with in excess of 50 each. Most of them offered a vast array of blackjack tables. The casinos prefer a player sign up for a player's card that requires furnishing personal identifying information including social security number. One benefit of a card is that a year-end printout can be provided to support a tax return in determining any tax owed due to net winnings. That's because all purchases and reimbursements of chips are recorded for blackjack players who sign up.

A player's card is the last thing a person wants to agree to if attempting to launder money is the primary goal. Laundering works only when a record of the purchase of chips is unknown to law enforcement. Turning chips back in for reimbursement wasn't a problem for Sam's scheme to work. In fact, he needed a record of that to be successful as part of his overall plan. An accurate record of purchasing chips, however, would negate any chance of utilizing this method of laundering.

At its most basic level, the strategy Sam intended to implement consisted of the following two steps: (1) Purchase chips with stolen funds to play at the blackjack table and (2) Turn the chips in at the cashier's cage for a check issued by the casino. The chips could be purchased with no personal information provided at either the cage or directly from the blackjack dealer depending on the amount involved. Sam could then claim he had won the money playing blackjack and thus convert the true origin of stolen funds into legitimate gambling profits.

His tax return for the year would end up disclosing the 1.5 million as a taxable gain. That meant he would have to pay Uncle Sam close to one third of the stolen money. Still, that left him close to 1 million to spend as he pleased. Assuming the blackjack ruse worked as planned, that meant he could openly display his newfound wealth and the FBI and anybody else could do little more than speculate his sudden prosperity had sprung from the cash in the armored car.

What would make the whole charade even sweeter was the alleged gambling winnings matched almost exactly the amount of the stolen money. Just like the FBI had known from the beginning he was the thief, they would have no doubt it was no innocent coincidence his claimed winnings closely matched the amount of the theft. But, having no uncertainty about something was a long way from establishing convincing evidence proving guilt beyond a reasonable doubt. If he didn't slip up along the way, there was no prosecuting attorney in any U.S. Attorney's office capable of obtaining an indictment, let alone convincing a jury, that the source of the money could be inextricably tied to the robbery.

The challenge now was it would take all the cunning, stealth and stamina he could muster to ensure he didn't slip up along the way. Ensuring neither the FBI nor the casinos became aware of the scam before all the money was washed was absolutely critical. Casinos were required to report any suspicious laundering activity to law enforcement and the penalty for not doing so was significant. So, not only did he need to keep the FBI in the dark for up to a year, but any suspicion on the part of the casino employees could prove painfully calamitous.

To keep the FBI in the dark as long as possible, he planned to deposit his casino checks in various different banks in and around Las Vegas. Hopefully, all these banks wouldn't be checked by the FBI to see if he was an account holder. The best outcome would be if the St. George RA somehow failed to include that as part of their investigative protocol. Still, it wouldn't be absolutely disastrous if they did discover the accounts since the deposits couldn't be tied directly to the theft. It would, however, get them closer to wondering exactly what he was up to and that would most likely lead to his plot being slightly more difficult to keep under wraps.

Keeping any casino in the dark for as long as possible was just as important. Sam needed to count cards at the blackjack tables as well as incorporating his other winning strategies in order to create the impression he had the capability of winning 1.5 million dollars. But, if the casinos caught on he was that good, they could team up to be on the lookout for him as an undesirable, thus posing one more obstacle in the way of the easy accessibility his plan hoped to achieve. Not only that, they might report him to law enforcement and that was the kind of attention he had to avoid.

He would play it by ear depending on the casino involved. Over a three or four day period, he would in most instances make several purchases of chips from both the blackjack tables and the central cage totaling no more than $10,000 from a single casino. He would then cash in half the chips purchased plus anymore he won on two separate occasions during that three or four day amount of time. He'd take his winnings in two checks issued by each casino to use a backup documentation when he filed his taxes.

Casino regulations required personal information to be obtained for any single purchase or reimbursement of $10,000 or more. Sam would make sure he never came anywhere close to succumbing to that requirement. Averaging smaller multiples totaling $10,000 each at 150 casinos spread throughout Nevada would take care of laundering the entire 1.5 million. The key to success would be keeping his playing at any one casino as inconspicuous as possible so as not to draw attention from employees trained to detect card sharks and money launderers. Let the fun begin.

SEVENTEEN

Samantha Diaz was a cocktail waitress at Planet Hollywood located just off the Strip. She was also an absolute knockout. Her father was a handsome native born Argentinean and her mother a gorgeous white female born in Las Vegas who had worked as a topless dancer in her earlier years. That combination of DNA had produced a daughter who was stunning by just about any standard of beauty imaginable.

Everything about her face was spectacular from her perfectly shaped nose, mesmerizing emerald green eyes, naturally colored dark eyebrows and rose tinted lips surrounding perfectly formed sparkling white teeth. She had distinctive cheekbones and an irresistible dimple that appeared when she flashed her infectious smile. All of this flawlessness was framed by thick and silky dark brown hair with a natural tint of auburn that appeared just as appealing sloppy wet from the shower as it did blown dry and arrestingly coiffured.

She was 29 years young, 5'4", and weighed a lithesome 120 lbs. From her neck down, her body uniquely distinguished itself as being exquisitely formed with appealing muscular definition on a slender small-boned frame. She worked out regularly but most of the perfection had most likely been inherited. Some people have all the luck. Her creamy light brown skin was imperfection free. She was one of those fortunate females who didn't require the sun to look spectacular. She looked almost as good getting out of bed in the morning as when she preened for a night on the town.

His master plan didn't include getting serious with a woman, but it was hard to resist a stunner like her. He had enjoyed a continuous diet of over-night trysts with numerous seductive females in the gaming business, and that had been the limit of how far he was presently willing to go. Mandy, however, made it hard to continue on within that frame of mind. She sexually excited him as no other women ever had and matched his enthusiasm for promiscuous experimentation and spontaneity.

More than pure sex, both seemed hooked at the hip as far as sharing many of the same interests and having similar convictions on topics like religion and politics. She filled a previously unrecognized need in him for companionship and emotional fulfillment. He felt completely as ease in her presence and looked forward to being with her more and more. The thought of discontinuing his relationship with her had slowly started to become a disconcerting option. Even though rationality hinted that was probably the wisest choice to make, he was having a harder and harder time thinking how empty his existence would feel if she was to suddenly disappear from his life.

Mandy confided she had been married twice. Her first abortive union lasted just over five years. It fell apart when her husband became a stumbling alcoholic who too often physically and mentally abused her when intoxicated. She finally filed for divorce and obtained a restraining order after he wouldn't leave her alone. Finally, after being arrested and convicted for breaking into her apartment in a drunken rage, he moved back east after being released from jail and she hadn't had any further contact with him going on more than four years now.

Her second marriage lasted less than two years and ended almost as badly as the first. He was a rich executive with a position high up in the gaming business. He was good looking and seemed like the perfect life partner at first. That turned out to be a cruel deception when he became unreasonably jealous even when she did nothing more than innocently flash her infectious smile at another man. He started to control practically every aspect of her life until she felt like she was a prisoner with no personal freedom to act on her own. She once again filed for divorce. She came away with nothing monetarily because of a pre-nuptial agreement he had insisted on.

She told Sam she had, like him, reverted to a life of one night stands to satisfy her sexual cravings, but had decided against any kind of serious romancing for the foreseeable future. He was the first man she had met in over two years now with whom she had continued to date over an extended period. She still wasn't ready to consider a third marriage, but her feelings for him had caused her to consider the possibility another serious relationship may not be completely off the table.

Both had just consummated an intensely erotic encounter with the sun shining brightly on her mostly hidden apartment balcony. With her wearing nothing more than a pair of dangling earrings and a red pair of ankle-wrapped high heels, they had spent the better part of an hour engaging in an exotic variety of sexual entanglements. Her involuntary moans and gasps based on two spectacular orgasms and almost a third could be heard by who knows how many people who may have been in close proximity.

Afterwards, wrapping herself in a sexy thigh high black silk robe, Mandy asked, "Exactly what are you planning to do with the rest of your life? Unless you plan to earn a living as a professional gigolo, which by the way I think you would be very successful at, how do you plan to financially survive when your unemployment checks run out? I know it's not my business but I have to wonder. Do you think you can survive on what you can win at the blackjack tables? You're good, but I don't know if anybody's that good. A girl who's starting to like you a lot can't help but wonder."

"I don't know Mandy. I guess I'll worry about that when the time comes. It's not going to be easy to find regular employment when anybody checks into my last job. You may not be giving me enough credit on my card playing prowess. As long as they don't catch me card counting, who knows how long I could go and how much I could come away with. Does that kind of uncertainly bother you? Is that why you're asking?

"It's really none of my business. It's your life. I'll admit recently I've done a little daydreaming about what it might be like if our time together was a little more permanent than our seemingly insatiable desire to fornicate. Then again, that's not a bad state of existence. Maybe, I don't really want anything more than that. Think you're up for one more round?

If he only knew the real Mandy, it would have undoubtedly cooled his libido.

EIGHTEEN

"Sounds like you may be getting closer to where he may slip up and admit something incriminating. That would be great for me and even better for you with the prospect of raking in a cool hundred grand." SA Cook was in the process of secretly debriefing Mandy in an out-of-the-way Las Vegas motel room he had secured for that purpose. They were evaluating her recent tryst on her apartment balcony.

"I don't know", she wondered. "Is he really a crook? He hasn't opened up yet if he is. I think he's starting to like me and even possibly thinking about something more than sex between the two of us, but nothing so far approaching sharing any admission of guilt. I did what you suggested and tried to confront him about his lack of a steady job and how he planned to get by. He didn't say anything about any kind of hidden stash. So far, I haven't seen any evidence of a ton of extra money. I just don't know."

She stood not only to benefit from the reward, but was being paid several hundred dollars each time she agreed to meet with Sam. She also received payment for any extra expenses she incurred while playing her role. So far, that had included money for some sexy outfits, jewelry, food and other furnishings to make her apartment appear to have been solely occupied by her. The budget even included her purchase of wine and liquor to help loosen Sam's tongue.

She was now an officially numbered FBI informant with an agreement to testify in front of a grand jury and in any court trial if it ever got that far. She wasn't concerned about revealing her identity or any potential for retribution on the part of her so far clueless target. Sam may be a diabolical thief, but she was sure he didn't have a threatening bone in his body.

"Don't be impatient," Steve cautioned. "These things sometimes take a while. I think you've made great headway. We may now be able to take a chance and wire your apartment for sound and video. When and if he admits anything, that would provide us with the best evidence. Your credibility couldn't be questioned if we can get that kind of collaboration. You'll easily be able to discreetly turn it off and on depending on the situation."

Wiring up an informant for sound was always the best way to go unless there was a good chance the body recorder might be discovered. Because of the frequent and random naked sexual encounters between the two, that option had been vetoed. Since he had shown absolutely no proclivity to check the apartment for bugs, that had now become a viable alternative with minimal likelihood of being detected.

"Good, that's a relief," Mandy sighed. "I'm obviously no prude, but the thought of having our sex on tape is a little farther than I'd like to go. What do I do if he starts to get really serious and offers me an engagement ring or something? I'm not so sure he may not be getting close to considering something like that."

"Let's cross that bridge when and if we ever get to it. I take it you're not in love with this guy. I guess if he wanted to get engaged, we could go along with it for a while. That kind of situation would obviously make it even more likely he may be willing to open up to you."

"Let me be clear about that," she emphasized. "The only interest I have in this whole deal is getting the reward. He seems like a nice guy and all that but I'm in love with someone else and he'll mean nothing more to me when this is all over than having a bunch more dinero and whatever that can buy."

Nothing that Mandy had confided to Sam was the truth. The majority of lies had been concocted between her and SA Cook prior to her meetings with the so far apparently clueless scammer. She had been successfully recruited as an informant using the reward money as a convincing enticement. Steve had been prepared to approach other casino cuties he had observed him cavorting with, but didn't have to when Mandy had enthusiastically agreed to sign up. She had been more successful than Steve could have ever hoped for in seducing him without seeming to have a hint about the trap into which he was tumbling.

Mandy was bi-sexual and could be just as erotically satisfied and orgasmic with men as with women. Right now, however, she was in love and deeply committed to a fellow cocktail waitress by the name of Julie who was a petite blond almost, but not quite, as stunningly attractive as Mandy. They lived together quite comfortably in an up-scale apartment within a short commute from Planet Hollywood. The combination of their incomes including above average tips due primarily to being so damned good looking made for a moderately comfortable lifestyle. Add in another $100,000 and it would be better than moderate.

Julie was all in and wasn't concerned about the extracurricular sexual activity with Sam. Both she and Mandy had an open relationship that allowed for outside sex when the urge presented itself. Their only rule was they practice safe sex and regularly be tested for STDs. The reality was that both of them had infrequently participated in group sexual encounters with people they knew well and trusted to be STD responsible.

Both agreed it was best to hide their close relationship from Sam. It wouldn't be disastrous if he found out but it could complicate things more than was necessary. He probably wouldn't go berserk if he found out Mandy was having a lesbian relationship. He didn't own her, but why complicate matters.

Julie agreed to move in with another co-worker for the interim until Mandy had completed her assignment. They concocted a phony excuse unrelated to the undercover operation. Julie would use her part of rent to apply to the apartment of her temporary roommate. Mandy had been assured the informant payments to her would cover the missing rent. Much of the personal relationship between Julie and Mandy would still take place in their apartment. They just had to use the upmost of caution not to cross paths with Sam.

The downside of her undercover (literally) work was that Mandy had to spend a significant amount of her off time continually plotting with the FBI. There was worry about him discovering her true motivation requiring she be constantly on guard of him inadvertently observing her doing anything suspicious when they were apart.

The upside, on the other hand, in addition to the possibility of a big score, was she had been pleasantly surprised the intrigue had actually proved exciting. She was enjoying her role that found her looking forward to the constantly unfolding drama.

NINETEEN

Becoming capable of realistically changing his appearance had been a key element of his master plan from the beginning. Not only might it help to frustrate surveillance attempts by the FBI and anyone else who may be interested in tracking his movements, but he figured it would be essential in preventing suspicious casino employees from reporting him as a possible card counter or money launderer.

His trip to Hollywood and the specialty store concentrating in magically altering actors' looks had proved fruitful. The cost of quality makeup and other materials hadn't been inexpensive to be sure, but investing just under $1,700 had allowed him to secure professional face and body altering gear that produced a truly naturalistic result.

In addition to quality makeup, he purchased the following additional items: (1) three different nose disguises you would swear were made of real flesh. A slight touch of makeup sealed the deal so it was likely no one but a professional movie makeup artist would suspect the modification, (2) two wigs including one with collar length hair and the other that created the realistic impression of being bald on top, (3) one mustache and a beard that were virtually undetectable, and (4) a protruding false gut that could be discretely hidden under a shirt and give the impression of needing to lose at least 40 lbs.

All these items were easily stored in a small gym bag that the FBI had discovered during their initial search of his residence. SA Hilton had quizzed Sam about the purpose of the bag and its contents. Sam had reminded Hilton he had been given legal advice not to answer any questions posed by law enforcement or anyone else for that matter. Unable to confiscate the bag because there was no logical tie to the robbery, there was little chance the changed appearance of Sam could be recognized at a later date. The mishmash of individual pieces of disguise paraphernalia would be almost impossible to subsequently identify him from his altered appearance.

Although it could put a definite dent in his plan if casinos prematurely figured out he was disguising his true identity before all the money was laundered, it wouldn't be quite as risky if the FBI found out unless they immediately shared that information with all the casinos Sam intended to visit. That was unlikely.

The use of disguises would prove to be of trivial consequence once the money was laundered. It would be too late for any of the casinos who might be interested in limiting his play. If it came up in court, he would simply explain he disguised himself to reduce the chance of being pegged as a habitual card counter. After all, there was nothing illegal about it. The preferred outcome, of course, was no one figuring out he was regularly changing his looks before all the stolen funds were safely laundered.

By mixing and matching the disguise materials with different clothes and hats, he figured he could persuasively alter his appearance in over a dozen different ways. He'd been practicing his makeup skills and was actually astounded how different he could make himself look. He saw what appeared to be a complete stranger when looking in the mirror. How much more difficult would it be for others to recognize his true identity if he had a hard time himself.

"I think I'm getting closer to busting the Sam Scam. There's no doubt he he's done an impressive job in covering his tracks so far, but he may be close to dropping his guard because of what appears to be his ever increasing infatuation over Mandy. She's really something. I can see myself as dropping my guard if I was in his place. She's one good looking babe to be sure."

SA Cook was briefing his new partner, SA Lytle, on his latest efforts to solve the armored car theft.

Tony responded, "How do you know you can trust her? Sure, she stands to gain a hundred grand, but he can offer her the benefit of a million and a half. What if they really do end up falling in love and she decides she would rather side with him than us. It could happen that way. It's something to consider don't you think?"

"Good point, but I just don't see it going down that way," Steve countered. "She would be risking being charged with criminal conspiracy and end up with nothing but a criminal record and probable time in the can. You never can tell for sure I guess, but I just don't peg her as the type to be willing to take that kind of chance. Besides, it's the best thing we've got going. Nothing else has worked out so far. About falling madly in love, I think Mandy is serious about her girlfriend and a lesbian relationship is all she's interested in right now."

"Falling in love or not," Tony challenged, "This dude hasn't come close yet to sharing his crime with her. I thought she did a good job in trying to get him to confide, but nothing came of it. What makes you think he ever will? He could marry her and still never share anything about the robbery."

"I suppose so, but think about how hard that would be to pull off. I mean, think how much sweeter it would be to share the intrigue with the one you love and trust. I can't imagine the willpower it would take to keep it all inside. She's no saint. If he comes to the conclusion she cares enough about their relationship not to be a risk, who's to say he won't succumb to the temptation to bring her into a two-person fold?

"Well, one thing's for sure," Tony readily agreed. "It seems to be the best chance for success, at least at this point in time. I guess all we can do is hope for the best and see what happens. I think the biggest risk is her being able to keep her undercover identity secret. This guy's no dope."

"That's for sure. Getting approval to rent different cars for surveillance may make a difference too. I'm pretty sure he had no idea I was following him the other day when he parked at New York New York in Vegas. Unfortunately, I lost him after he got out of the car. I checked the casino but he wasn't at any of the blackjack tables. He showed up a few hours later, but I have no idea where he might have been. I stayed way back so he wouldn't make me. I could barely see him. I've got to figure a way to get closer. Maybe you can help out next time and we'll have more luck with two of us tailing him."

TWENTY

The cleansing was about to commence! Sam was preparing to begin the laundering of the first approximately $50,000 of his 1.5 million stash. He figured it would take somewhere between three and four days to take this initial step to convert cash to chips. First, he planned to purchase chips in the amount of about $5,000 from each of five casinos over a several hour period. Several days later, he would return to the same casinos and purchase chips for another $5,000 each.

A decision was made to start with casinos where he hadn't previously played blackjack. The five he chose were the Vegas Club located along the Fremont Street Experience, Arizona Charlie's in West Las Vegas, The Palms west of the Strip, Sam's Town in East Vegas, and Palace Station on the west side of I-15. They were chosen because he wanted to stay off the Strip to start. He didn't expect the FBI had any idea about his strategy, but a super cautious approach at first was to stay away from the most obvious Strip casinos where he frequented and had most likely been followed.

Of the more than two hundred casinos in Nevada, slightly fewer than eighty were located in Las Vegas. Sam planned to stay as close to this gambling mecca as possible. The only exceptions would be if it appeared any of the casinos seemed unduly suspicious about his play. He felt somewhat gifted at being able to diagnose even the smallest hint of physical mannerisms indicating a dealer or another casino employee might be in the process of singling him out for special attention.

Since he had estimated it would take a total of approximately 150 casinos to safely complete the task, he knew he was going to have to eventually spread out around the rest of Nevada. Although he preferred not to, he was willing to go out of Nevada if required. California and Oklahoma were the two most likely target states if that became necessary.

Any extra expenses for travel would most likely require use of his true identity and a credit card. Planes, car rentals and most decent motels required it. The extra spending wasn't a problem as far as appearing to directly include part of the stolen money, since he had large available credit card balances requiring only minimum monthly payments. What he wanted to avoid, if possible, was sparking unnecessary questions about the purpose behind an expanded travel itinerary while he was supposedly handicapped by a tight budget.

Although the vast majority of federal investigation would take place in Nevada, it didn't follow that Nevada FBI agents less familiar with the case would be covering all the possible leads. For the most part, the best plan of attack would be for SAs Cook and/ or Lytle to make the relatively short trip from St. George involving frequent trips to Las Vegas. That was due to their extensive background knowledge of Sam's activities. They could still request Nevada reinforcements when needed, but it was better office of origin agents maintain on-site surveillance when at all feasible.

SA Cook had recently requested the specialized Las Vegas surveillance team, almost identical in makeup to the Salt Lake City team, assist in following Sam as he made one of his numerous trips to the Strip. The specialized team including a plane was set to go when Sam pulled into the above ground parking lot at the Bellagio. But, by the time the team could reconfigure to the parking lot, he had mysteriously disappeared into the massive labyrinth formed by dozens of casinos, enumerable entrances and exits, and the ever present flood of out-of-town visitors.

The plane proved to be of no value. There had been some reluctance to use it in the first place because of the close proximity to the often congested McCarran International Airport. An initial check of every nook and cranny of the Bellagio failed to find any trace of the illusive target. After just under three hours of a wasted surveillance effort, he finally returned to pick up his car from where he drove directly back to his apartment in St. George. The Las Vegas team had hit a disappointing dead end just as had been the case with the Salt Lake team.

Steve wasn't about to request more assistance from the always busy Las Vegas division unless he felt there was a better than even chance of success. The Vegas office was one of the busiest in the FBI. Most of the agents were burdened with a stack of case files often requiring a considerable amount of overtime devotion. Agents were paid a regular 25% bonus for overtime work covering an extra 10 hours a week. Anything over that was work not normally reimbursed. Most Las Vegas agents worth their salt ended up working considerably more than a 50 hour week. Cook didn't want to add to that unnecessarily.

The truth was the more Steve and Tony tried to follow him, the more they realized it was pretty much becoming as waste of time. Even with an FBI approved rental car, it appeared he was constantly tail conscious and took effective steps to preclude any kind of successful surveillance no matter who was following him or what they might be driving.

After a frustrating period fast approaching a year since the theft, the two agents were starting to finally accept the harsh reality surveillance, no matter how proficient the following team might be, was most probably not going to be the key to solving the case. Donahue was simply turning out to be too cagey to be compromised in that fashion. Additionally, Las Vegas was too crowded and offered too many ways for even the most obtuse of targets to evade being followed. Sam had proven himself to be anything but dense in adroitly covering his tracks.

Cook had concluded the best chance for success at the present time was Mandy would come through with getting Sam to say something incriminating and be recorded. Even though nothing approaching that had yet to occur, the relationship between them seemed to getting closer and closer. It wouldn't be the first time the lust for a women had caused otherwise cautious subjects to lose their objectivity.

Other than Mandy and a continuing close watch on Sam's financial dealings, Cook had little more to go on at this late date. Surely, something positive would soon break through the continuing quagmire.

TWENTY-ONE

Anyone knowledgeable of the master plan might accuse the creator of being overly cautious and well on the road to full-blown paranoia. Sam didn't see it that way. There was far too much on the line to lower his guard this late in the game and make some stupid mistake landing him behind bars and negating all his previously crafted precautions. At this critical juncture, successfully laundering the cash was going to require even greater attention to detail in order not to derail his scheme in midstream.

The first obstacle he had needed to resolve was how to safely travel to and from the shed he had rented in Las Vegas. It was critical to get this part of his plan right because he contemplated making over a hundred such trips to and from the shed in order to launder the entire 1.5 million. Success by the FBI in linking him to the shed would risk bringing down the whole operation. Enough probable cause to get a search warrant to search the shed would guarantee discovering his intermediate stash location.

His plan for all these trips would be essentially the same. He would park his car in one of the free high rise casino parking lots on the Strip. From there, he would walk several blocks in an attempt to lose anyone who may be following. He would then use public transportation and/or a cab to deliver him to a location a few blocks from where he had rented the apartment. After walking to the apartment, he would disguise his appearance and proceed to the shed in the Toyota purchased in New Mexico.

The shed would not only be used to hide the cash, but the same hiding spots in the desk and file cabinets would be required to also conceal the 1.5 million worth of chips he intended to purchase with the cash and finally the same dollar amount of casino checks he intended to obtain after cashing in the chips. No doubt about it, the shed had to remain a carefully guarded secret. All the laundering activity would revolve around it.

After each segment of the plan to launder part of the cash, he would return to the shed, drop off the chips and/or checks, proceed to the apartment, remove the disguise, and walk a few blocks away where he would utilize public transportation and/or a cab to return to within walking distance of his car in the casino parking lot.

The master plan envisioned washing $25,000 a night using five casinos. He would return to the same five casinos several weeks later wearing a different disguise and launder an additional $25,000 for a total of $50,000 at each grouping of five casinos. That would require about 30 groupings of 5 casinos each for a total of 150 casinos to cleanse the entire 1.5 million.

Since $25,000 in cash or the same amount in chips would be difficult to conceal, he planned to return to the Toyota in-between each casino stop to get more cash or store chips. He had already concocted a hiding space under the front passenger seat to temporarily store the cash and/or chips. He didn't worry much about theft. The older Toyota wasn't exactly a car thief's dream and anybody breaking into the car would most likely fail to discover the hidden compartment.

He planned to use 50 and 100 dollar bills to purchase chips in the same amounts. Since much of the stolen funds were in denominations of 5, 10 and 20 dollars, he planned to cash them in for 50s and 100s at banks, retail outlets, and/or casino teller cages surrounding the five he had selected to launder the money.

Once inside each casino, he would spend about 1½ hours at different blackjack tables while purchasing a total of about $5,000 worth of chips. He would make purchases at both the tables and the teller's cage so none of the separate purchases exceeded $1000. This time he would use all of his skills to win as much as he could. No more trying to lose a few so that he wouldn't become suspect of card counting. He hoped to win enough to put a dent in covering the taxes he was going to have to pay to Uncle Sam.

There was some minimal danger that dealers and cage personal would become suspicious about buying chips with cash in fairly large amounts several times during a relatively short period of time. For that reason, he would try to make sure none of those selling him chips noticed him buying them from someone else. Although a certain amount of suspicion may begin to mount, Sam felt he could leave before his play became suspect. With his disguises in place, he considered the risk of his scheme being successfully derailed as negligible.

Since there was no time limit to cash in the chips, Sam planned to hold off doing so until toward the end of the year, most probably in late October or early November. There was no reason to prematurely show his hand while he was still laundering the money. Once all the money was turned into chips, he would return twice, separated by at least a day, to each of the casinos. He would cash in approximately half of the chips each day ending up with two separate checks from each casino payable to his true name for a total of $10,000 in washed funds plus hopefully more depending on his skill as a player.

He figured returning twice to each of the approximately 150 casinos to cash in the chips would take a total of no more than 15 minutes each. He estimated it would take no more than 2-3 weeks to complete this part of the plan. As an extra precaution, he would try to make sure he never cashed in his chips twice with the same cashier. That wouldn't be that hard since most cashiers worked no more than an eight hour shift. Cashing in once in the morning and the next time in the evening should solve that problem nicely. Doing so two separate days would be risking even less.

Obtaining two checks on separate days payable to his true name in the approximate amount of $5,000 plus each shouldn't set off any alarms. It was a single transaction in the amount of $10,000 or more that seemed to get management's attention. Winning more chips may require a third day of cashing in chips to avoid that possibility.

TWENTY-TWO

Now about half way through laundering the money, Sam would need to dig up the remaining 3 drums. He would conduct that retrieval essentially the same way he had done it the first time with the only difference being he planned to rent a vehicle in Las Vegas this time.

He realized that the jeep he planned to rent from a discount rental agency in Vegas would require he provide his true name and his Visa card also listing in his name. That meant the FBI would soon thereafter find out from his credit card account he had rented the jeep. That wouldn't be a problem in his estimation since the discovery would almost certainly come far too late to initiate a successful tail. The time from initial rental to the safe storage of the cash would be just under two hours. This would be the only rental initiated as part of the master plan.

After all the money was cleaned, the checks then totaling the full 1.5 million plus would be hidden in the shed in place of the cashed-in chips. He would wait until the last two weeks in December to begin depositing the checks to a dozen different checking accounts he had previously established. The checks remained negotiable for up to six months so that wouldn't pose a problem. What might cause somewhat of a stir was the depositing of close to 300 separate casino checks in the amount of about $5,000 plus each. That would result in total deposits of approximately $125,000 plus per bank.

Since none of the deposits were being made with cash, the banks wouldn't be required to file a Currency Transaction Report (CTR) to law enforcement authorities. By depositing the checks over a couple of weeks in several smaller increments, that meant his laundering activities would hopefully remain hidden from the FBI until sometime after he filed his 2015 tax return which would then result in a sudden bomb shell of unexpected investigative upheaval.

The IRS would exit the scene once Sam paid them the tax in early February, 2016 on the entire 1.5 million plus. They would obviously be curious why he had not offset that amount with any loses he most likely would have incurred in the normal course of gambling. They might well be befuddled, but that would be about the extent of it. They would have obtained the maximum amount of tax possible to recover and there would be no reason to investigate any further.

SAs Cook and Lytle, on the other hand, would have absolutely no doubt whatsoever the 1.5 million plus deposited tied directly to the same amount their cagey target had embezzled. Sam envisioned the look of consternation on their faces as they marveled he had so blatantly deposited the stolen money right in front of their noses. The problem would be they'd have no evidence beyond a reasonable doubt to tie the missing money to the deposits.

Anyway, that was the way the master plan was intended to play out. He was still confident but a long way off from final success. The next few months would determine if his optimism had been well founded or if the FBI had somehow figured a way to trip up their ever-irritating protagonist.

"I can't think of anything else to say that won't make him suspicious of my questioning. He has yet to volunteer even a hint he stole the money or even that he has extra money he's been sitting on. I don't know what else I can say or do to open him up." Mandy was obviously becoming frustrated as she plotted her deception with SA Cook in a motel room not far from the FBI office in St. George.

"The worst thing you can do right now, Mandy, is become discouraged. These things often take a while to produce results. The simple fact you've been successful in developing a meaningful relationship with the primary suspect in the theft is amazing and a real stroke of luck for us as investigators. You're the best thing we've got going right now. Without you, we've pretty much hit a dead end. The worst thing that could happen would be for you to give up."

"I appreciate your confidence but you keep coaching me to talk about things that might get him to say something incriminating. He's no dope. If I keep on doing that, he's bound to become suspicious. I'm becoming a nervous wreck I'm going to slip and say something that's going to tip him off. I don't think I'm in any kind of danger or anything like that. It's just I don't see where this is going anywhere."

"I get your frustration," Cook sympathetically responded. "I think you may be right about pressing too much. It may be better to just let things go as they are for a while and see what happens on its own. Hopefully, he'll feel comfortable enough with you in the not too distant future to let something slip or even better decide he wants someone close to him to share in his deception. Do you have any problem proceeding in that manner?"

"I guess not. That will make it a lot easier on me. I can't complain about the money you've been paying me and the possibility of the reward. I'll give it another month or two. After that, I think it may be time to get back to my real life. This is getting a little bit old to tell you the truth; especially, if it becomes apparent the chance of opening him up has realistically become nothing more than a pipe dream."

"Fair enough," Cook agreed. "In fact, I think you are exactly right in your concern. I agree we probably need to pull you out if we can't see any positive results in that amount of time. I've still got one or two things we might try. Let me do some more thinking on it before I share them with you. For now, let's just make sure you try to keep his trust so that your relationship can continue to flourish."

"One other small matter," Mandy concluded. "Would it be possible to have these meetings in Vegas from now on? It would make it easier on my job."

"No problem. Las Vegas it is from here on out. Thanks for agreeing to stick it out a while longer. Hopefully, we'll see more positive results sooner than later."

TWENTY-THREE

Mandy's concern with Sam finding out about her true intentions was closer to reality than she might have imagined. It started when he caught a glimpse of her in a secluded area of Planet Hollywood with a co-worker who he later learned was named Julie. Unobserved by the two, he witnessed them engage in a quick kiss on the mouth. In and of itself, he didn't think that much about it. After all, friends do kiss each other on occasion although it usually isn't on the mouth.

Even if it was more than that, he didn't have the right to dominate her personal life. He had been thinking about the possibility of asking her to marry him, but that hadn't happened yet. Maybe she liked girls as well as boys when it came to her sexual orientation. He didn't have a big problem with that either. What did bother him a little was they had been getting pretty serious and being intimate with someone else, whether it be male or female, seemed somewhat of a lover's betrayal.

Then, he started to think about several instances where Mandy had seemed overly concerned about him losing his job and how he planned to earn a living other than by relying on winning at blackjack. She swore she backed him 100 percent when he thought he had convinced her he had been robbed. But, what if she hadn't been? What if it was some kind of act she was putting on? What if she thought he had the money and was less enamored with him and more interested in somehow capitalizing on what she suspected might be a potential source of a higher standard of living?

And then it hit him. What about the possibility she'd been co-opted by law enforcement or someone else to get close to him and get evidence he'd stolen the money. He now admitted to himself, as careful as he had been in anticipating every other potential dilemma that could upset his master plan, he hadn't been anywhere near as vigilant in vetting Mandy. He'd been infatuated with her from the beginning and was now for the first time wondering if he could have been blinded by pure lust. After all, she was an amazing and mesmerizing woman.

Although he still thought it unlikely she had any ulterior motives, he decided he'd been super cautious with everything else and it might be wise to continue that same level of precaution when it came to his new true love. He'd been followed continuously for months now. Maybe it was time to do a little surveillance on his own. He decided to spend the better part of a week to see what she was up to when she wasn't with him.

The first thing catching his attention was when he saw Julie and her holding hands while walking from Planet Hollywood to her apartment. Even those who are just friends normally don't walk for blocks holding hands. Again, he didn't have a big problem with that as far as sexual preference goes, but it did somewhat concern him she may be having some kind of affair when she had been repeatedly assuring him he was the only current love interest in her life.

Several days later, he followed her taking a cab to a one-story medium priced motel about a mile from Planet Hollywood. He observed her enter a motel room by herself and exit about 45 minutes later. She got in a cab and drove away. Instead of continuing to follow her, he decided to sit on the motel room and determine who may still be in the room. It shocked him when a few minutes later he recognized SA Cook leaving the room and getting into the car he realized was the same vehicle that had followed him on numerous previous occasions.

His immediate inclination was to give Mandy the benefit of the doubt. Maybe he just wanted to interview her about the obvious relationship Cook had observed developing between her and Sam. His surveillance could easily have picked up on that. There was no reason to immediately conclude she was cooperating with him in any kind of undercover operation. Perhaps, he was making an effort to recruit her, but it didn't automatically follow she had been willing to engage in such a deception.

He didn't want to believe she had or would consider turning against him, but his better judgment told him it would be naive not to consider otherwise. Why would they be meeting in an out-of-the-way motel room? If he just wanted to interview her, why not have done so at work or at her apartment afterwards? Sneaking around at a motel stunk of something much more threatening.

Could it possibly be he had interviewed her in the normal course of business, but that initial contact had ballooned into a full-blown illicit relationship? That possibility wasn't out of the question. Sam had pretty much fallen head over heels for her shortly after they first met. Maybe it wasn't all that illicit. He had just assumed Cook was married, but maybe he wasn't. It probably wouldn't be the first time an unmarried agent had fallen for a witness.

Regardless of what was really going on between Mandy and the FBI agent who was investigating him, it was now apparent he had to be more circumspect in his relationship with her. Luckily, he couldn't recall saying anything to her that could be used as evidence against him. So, even if she had been wired and all the conversations between the two of them had been recorded, he couldn't think of a single instance where he had incriminated himself.

That was because, as smitten as he had been with her, he had stuck with his first rule of thumb to ensure he wasn't caught; that being to make sure he was the only one who knew the truth of the illusion he had so carefully crafted. He would never have told her the truth even if he had ended up marrying her. There were just too many crooks that had been caught when a previously faithful spouse had turned on the other after an acrimonious divorce or for any number of other vengeful or self-serving reasons.

For now, he would let things ride like they were, but he would be even more cautious in his interactions with her. What the heck? She was still an insatiably terrific lay, and he would definitely miss that if he was to dump her now. Still, what a potential disappointment. The chance of any lasting relationship between the two was now very likely a dream gone awry.

TWENTY-FOUR

It was the middle of August and nobody with any sense was spending much time outside unless forced to because of their job or they were frolicking in the pool. St. George was experiencing an exceptionally hot spell averaging well over a hundred degrees, but Las Vegas was insane. It didn't take but a few minutes to begin sweating profusely while walking outside along the Strip. Sidewalk cold water plastic bottle hucksters were selling out on every block.

The only plus making life bearable in this gambling mecca was the magnificent volume of refreshing air conditioning permeating every square inch of every casino. It was hard to imagine the total utility bill for all these mammoth structures devoted to the risk takers who swarmed to test their luck while easily covering the cost of cooling.

As much as Sam patronized the blackjack tables during these scorching summer months, most reputable psychologists might reasonably label him as a gambling addict. An addict no less so than those addicted to alcohol, pornography, smoking, drugs or any of the other vices destructively controlling people's lives. As far as his perceived addictive proclivity was concerned, such a judgment couldn't be further from the truth.

Smoking to him was disgusting. Not only because it created an unnecessary health risk, but because it took over control of a person's life. He tried it only once when a cute girl in high school dared him to take a puff. That was the last puff he ever took. The thought of willingly succumbing to such a filthy and expensive habit was a sign of weakness running counter to his very core values. He was never even slightly tempted to try illegal drugs.

Addictive behavior was simply not part of his makeup. He consumed alcohol responsibly while exhibiting none of the markers of an alcoholic. He never craved a drink early in the day. A couple of bottles of beer while watching a football game or a single mixed drink to be sociable was about as far as he cared to venture. He appreciated a little bit of a buzz from a glass of wine in anticipation of a good meal. It made him appreciate the taste of the food even more, but that was it. The idea of going beyond that and becoming regularly besotted was not something his body craved.

Drinking while gambling was an absolute no-no. That's what a casino hoped for. That's why all the cute honeys in short skirts plied serial players with free cocktails. That was the game plan. It was what they were trained to do. He needed his full faculties to perform his magic. The last thing he required was a free drink to dull his finely honed craft.

The same went with pornography. Soft porn in moderation was no big deal. Most of the good movies were R rated. What he wasn't was one of those guys who spent hours on end on the internet switching from one porn site to the next, consumed with lust and seemingly unable to think about anything else. In other words, he wasn't an addict along those lines any more than he was addicted to anything else.

He demanded complete restraint in every part of his living. It was in his nature not to allow anything that might diminish that control. The same level of moderation applied to playing blackjack. A gambling addict was someone whom casino owners craved. Such persons couldn't harness their play. An addict kept on playing until he lost everything he had won and then lost more, much more. An addict seemed incapable of admitting his temporary mastery of the game had limits.

He could easily disassociate himself with the blackjack table at any point in time if he thought he was beginning to act like an addict. If he wasn't absolutely confident he could win more than lose, he could have easily dropped playing cards without a second thought. To even consider the slight possibility gambling was taking control of his life would have nauseated his very being. He played it because he was a winner. Gambling didn't control him. He controlled it.

The master plan was proceeding right on schedule. He had easily laundered the first $750,000 and replaced the bills with fifty and one hundred dollar chips from approximately 150 casinos, most of which were a located in the immediate Las Vegas area. It had required some additional travel within Nevada, mostly in Reno. Needing to travel outside the state most probably wasn't now going to be required.

Not only had he been able to successfully cleanse the stolen money, but he had won a little over $150,000 more on his own and converted that amount to chips as well. Just last week, he had successfully removed the remaining stolen funds from the hole in the ground. He was glad he had rented the jeep, because he had passed a few cars going up and back on the dirt road. The rental had blended into the scenery a lot better than a sedan. He drove an extra 100 miles to make it harder to try to figure his actual destination.

Now safely hidden in the shed were chips totaling about 1.65 million. He had made sure to pay his rent in cash on both the shed and the apartment well in advance of when it was due. There were no signs of any undue interest on the part of neither the apartment nor shed managers. He had run into surrounding apartment tenants infrequently and their only reaction to him had been a polite but uninterested nod. They probably couldn't identify him in a lineup.

His makeup and disguises had proven to conceal his true identity better than he could have hoped. Maybe he would consider going into the business when this was all over. He could probably make good money along the strip. Applying makeup and wigs to gorgeous dancing girls might be fun. As far as he could tell, no one so far had glanced at him in a way indicating they suspected he was trying to hide his appearance.

Next on the agenda was to revisit the same casinos while making sure to look like a different player than the first time through. He had kept a small notebook to identify which appearance he had previously used. In case anybody ever got hold of the notebook, he used indecipherable codes that meant nothing to anyone but himself.

Yes, it was hot in Nevada but everything was cool. No hitches so far. All he had to do was to keep doing what he had been doing and never get so confident he let his guard down, not even for a minute.

TWENTY-FIVE

"Believe me; I can understand your frustration. I've just received some information that might encourage you to stay in a little while longer. The insurance agency for the armored car company has agreed to up their reward money to $150,000 dollars. Of course, I couldn't tell them about our relationship, but I indicated we weren't that far away from a possible breakthrough and could use a little more inspiration to keep our best option going. They readily agreed to raise the ante, but added that was as far as they were willing to go."

Mandy and SA Cook were meeting in the room of a Motel 6 not far from where she worked. She had just informed him she was just about ready to pull the plug. Sam had said nothing that could be used against him and she now had a hard time envisioning the time when he ever would.

"I guess that's good news," she responded unenthusiastically. "The trouble is it wouldn't matter if it was a million dollars if he never incriminates himself. I'm about to the point where I've finally convinced myself the reward money is a lost cause. I've gone this far because I really thought it might be possible, but I don't think so anymore. My roommate wants to move back in. She's not getting along that well with her temporary roommate. I think it may be about time to get back to normal."

"What do you think about the possibility of him offering you a ring and bringing you in on the scheme after that? Do you think there's a chance of that still happening?" He was trying to come up with something to keep her involved. He could feel her use as a productive informant quickly slipping away.

"I used to think so. Not so much anymore. I can't exactly put my finger on it. He hasn't really said anything about having any interest in breaking up, but it's been awhile now since he's hinted about getting more serious. I don't know why it is, but my best guess the chance is now much more unlikely. I think we came close, but the time may have come to give it up. I just don't think it's going to happen."

"I've got one more thing we might want to try before we give up." He hadn't wanted to bring it up, but he could tell she was about ready to close shop unless he came up with something more dramatic than continuing on the same path with the hope Sam would eventually confide in her. "If this doesn't work, we could end it. What would you say about that?"

"I guess it would depend on what you're talking about. I can't think of anything we haven't already tried."

"What would you think about a call to Sam saying you've been kidnaped and demanding half of the stolen money? We would take care of everything involving the extortion. All you would have to do is get lost for a few days. If he ended up forking over $750,000 or even admitting he had that much money in any way, the U.S. Attorney's office has indicated that would give us enough for an indictment. There's no way he could explain having that much extra cash. If it results in a successful prosecution, you would be eligible for the full reward. What do you think about that?"

"Wow, I have no idea if something like that might work. I have my doubts, but who knows? I guess I would be willing to go along, but I don't know how you can expect me to disappear. I'm not interested in risking losing my job. If that's what your suggesting, I guess my answer would be no."

"No, nothing like that," Steve assured her. Actually, he would have loved if she had offered to do that, but he was prepared to suggest another alternative. "I don't like to do it, but I'd be willing to sit down with you and your supervisor and bring her in on what we're trying to do. We would ask her to pretend you hadn't contacted her and she had no explanation for your absence. Of course, she wouldn't have to pay you for the few days you didn't show. We would cover that lost salary plus what you normally make on tips. Think your boss might go along with something like that?

"I guess we could try. She's always been a great supervisor. That's one main reason I don't want to lose my job. I think she likes me a lot. I get more favorable comments from customers than almost anyone else. We do have a couple of girls who substitute on a regular basis for one reason or another."

"Think we could trust her to keep what we're doing to the three of us"

"I think so. She's never been one to gossip. Most of us have felt free to confide in her without her telling anyone else. She's been really good that way."

It was two days later Mandy had arranged for a private meeting to include her supervisor, Barbara, along with both her and Steve. They had decided to take a little bit of a chance and meet with Barbara in her small office in a well hidden section of Planet Hollywood. Mandy had recently talked to Sam who told her he planned to be in Reno playing blackjack until late into the night.

Cook didn't tell Barbara everything. Simply, that Mandy had been working an important case on behalf of the FBI, and it would be very helpful if she could have a few days off. He emphasized it would be advantageous if she could simply respond to Mandy's co-workers and anyone else who might ask that she hadn't heard from her and was becoming slightly concerned about why she hadn't reported for work. He apologized for not being able to clue her in further, but hoped she appreciated that was as far as he could go for now.

At first, Barbara suggested she should probably bring her supervisor in on what was going on. Finally, Cook was able to convince her the fewer who knew the better. She finally agreed to keep it to herself as long as it didn't take too long and preferably no longer than a week. Cook assured her it wouldn't and now felt more at ease with Mandy's positive assessment of her ability to maintain confidentiality.

TWENTY-SIX

"Well it's done," Steve confirmed. "To be honest, I think it will be a miracle if it works. Mandy seems to be handling her temporary situation pretty well. I talked to her this morning. I think she's actually enjoying her brief respite up north. I expect Sam's going to be getting the ransom notice anytime now. I really have no idea how he might respond. What's your take, my man?" Steve and Tony were sitting on pins and needles as they consumed the first of what would end being several cups of coffee while wondering what might happen next.

"I have no idea," Tony responded. "My guess is he may imagine any different number of things stopping us in our tracks. It certainly wouldn't shock me if he figures us out and that will be the end of it. If he decides it's a real kidnaping, it's hard to know how he may react. He could suspect she has crossed him and is part of the extortion. He may very well care more about the money than her. I guess we won't get a hint until the phone call."

Both SAs had spent the previous day trying to decide exactly how to execute their extortion fabrication. They had decided to store Mandy in a Ramada Inn in Salt Lake City. It had taken longer to decide whether to initially make a telephone call to Sam or send an extortion letter. They had finally settled on a letter.

The ransom note using newspaper print pasted onto a piece of white paper read, "WE KNOW YOU STOLE THE MONEY. WE ONLY WANT HALF. STUFF A DUFFLE BAG WITH $750,000 AND WAIT FOR A CALL. WE'RE WATCHING YOU. ANY ATTEMPT TO CONTACT THE COPS AND YOU'LL NEVER SEE MANDY ALIVE AGAIN." The note had been placed between the screen door and the locked front door of his St. George apartment while Sam's car was parked in Las Vegas.

The follow up call would be made at night sometime in the next couple of days when they were sure he was back at his apartment. If, by a stroke of luck, he agreed to give up the money, they would direct him to proceed immediately to a pay telephone for further instructions. He would be then taken down at the phone booth with the hope the bag of money was in his car.

They had decided not to attempt to follow him prior to that time because he had been so successful in discovering previous surveillance attempts. They didn't want to take a chance of him figuring the FBI may somehow be involved in the kidnaping and then deciding to abort.

The recorded call came a day later at exactly 10pm when surveillance had placed him back in his apartment. A machine was used to disguise the voice of a Salt Lake City SA who was at the Ramada with Mandy.

Agent: "Have you got the money?"

Sam: "I'm not giving you anything until I know if Mandy is OK."

Agent: "Don't worry. She's fine. Follow our instructions and she's got nothing to worry about. If you don't, you'll never see her again."

Sam: "I want to talk to her before I do anything else."

Mandy: "Sam, I'm scared. Please don't let them kill me." (Phone yanked away from her)

Agent: "Enough! Now, are you ready to save your girlfriend?"

Sam: "I don't know who you are or why you think I might have that kind of money. I'm unemployed. Somebody has sold you a bill of goods. I'd have to win the lottery to come up with that much dough. If you're smart, you'll let her go and cut your losses. Give it up! You're wasting your time with me." Sam hung up.

The first thing he had done after receiving the note was to go to Planet Hollywood to see if he could locate Mandy. She wasn't working during what would have been her normal schedule. He finally got one of her co-workers to share that nobody knew why she wasn't there and it wasn't like her not to check in if she was sick or for any other reason. One thing was for sure. She was missing and the circumstances of that sudden disappearance were unknown to those closest to her.

He had already decided he wasn't going to go along with the extortion. He just wanted to talk to her to listen to the demeanor of her voice to see if it might provide a clue as to the authenticity of the alleged kidnaping. He couldn't tell one way or the other. The other reason for responding to the call was to get his claim of guiltlessness on tape if he was by chance being recorded.

His best guess was she wasn't in any danger of being killed. The fact he had observed her meeting with SA Cook was one reason for feeling that way. Her attempts to question him about his future financial prospects added additional fuel to his doubt.

In the end, he had concluded the extortion was more likely a ruse than a real kidnaping. The truth of the matter was he would have decided the same way even if he had determined the extortion was possibly authentic. Even then, he felt the likelihood of killing her was minimal. Threatening murder is a lot easier than foolishly committing it and subjecting the perpetrator to the death penalty with no further chance of benefitting financially.

He had decided against taking the threat to the FBI. The last thing he wanted was to become embroiled in a situation where they could extensively question him and possibly end up getting him to accidentally say something they could use against him. He meant it when he said his first and last conversation with law enforcement was when he furnished his initial signed statement.

Succumbing to the extortion even if authentic would have violated the cornerstone of his master plan. The most important part of his plan would have been demolished. All his careful efforts to date could have collapsed around him. Everything he had already successfully accomplished and was yet to hopefully achieve depended on him keeping his larceny to himself. That meant no one including potential kidnappers could ever know the truth. Absolute isolation was the cardinal rule that couldn't be broken under any conceivable circumstance.

TWENTY-SEVEN

Still hot, but starting to moderate a little in the evening hours, it was the middle of September in Las Vegas. Sam was down to the final rounds of converting cash to chips. Although he should have been ecstatic the most challenging segment of his transition had proceeded without a hitch, he was somewhat sad his romance with Mandy was no more. There had been a point where he had come close to convincing himself she was the girl of his dreams. She had proven to be so perfect in so many ways.

He was relieved, although not all that surprised, to determine she hadn't been harmed when he finally cornered her leaving work a couple of days after he had hung up on the alleged kidnapper. She let him know right up front she never had any real feelings for him. She had courted him for no other reason than to act undercover on behalf of the FBI. She was not interested in seeing him again. She had a whole life to catch up on that didn't include him. She even had the nerve to appear offended he had deserted her had the extortion been bona fide.

He felt both somewhat slow-witted and partially vindicated at the same time. He was a little shocked his undisciplined lustfulness had resulted in misreading her true intentions for as long as he had. He felt partially absolved by having lifted his blinders just in the nick of time to consider funny business may be afoot. Oh well, life goes on. It was a lesson on caution taken to heart. Hopefully, someday, not again during this critical juncture of his plan, he might rekindle a similar flame with someone who actually cared for him.

Right now, he had plenty to keep his mind fully occupied. In another few weeks, he would be initiating the third stage of the laundering process as he converted his cache of chips to individual casino checks. After that, the final stage when the checks would be deposited among various banks in and around the gaming capital. He wasn't yet out of the woods by any means. Intensified circumspection was the mantra by which he needed to continually remind himself.

Although nothing had happened so far to derail his carefully conceived plot, there was an event that occurred the week before causing him to momentarily experience a brief bout of unnerving trepidation and self-doubt. It started with a horrific nightmare in the middle of the night waking him in a cold sweat and increased heartbeat that didn't abate for several minutes; even after he realized it was only a dream and didn't reflect any part of reality. An unsettling feeling and fitful sleep continued until morning.

The dream had somehow located him alone on the wrong side of town in a strange city just as it was starting to turn dark. The more he tried to extricate himself from the predicament, the more wrong turns he encountered. His precarious situation worsened as a nearby gang of thugs begin to first notice and then slowly follow him from behind. Finally, he found himself cornered in a dead end alley with a high chain link fence. As he tried to climb the fence, two of the bloodthirsty thugs grabbed on to his pant legs and begin pulling him down. That's when he awoke.

Although the dream had nothing to do with his master plan, the mood it created throughout the morning hours caused him to wonder for the first time if he may be in over his head. What if he did get caught? What if he did get sent to a prison where he had to deal with gangs? Regardless, could he really withstand being confined even in a white collar correctional institution where personal safety wasn't a big issue?

Was he truly prepared to spend some of the still remaining and most productive years of his life being incarcerated? If he did go to prison, what would his life be like when he got out? Obviously, getting any kind of decent job would be out of the question. Could he exist on playing blackjack or would the casinos get together and ban him in some massive joint effort? Would disguises solve that problem? Did he really want to spend much of the rest of his life wearing disguises?

He could pick up the phone and call the FBI that very afternoon. Since he hadn't spent any of the money, he could hopefully negotiate a lesser charge and possibly obtain a probated sentence while agreeing to perform community service. He would agree to attend any kind of corrective counseling dictated by the court. He could hide the extra money he had won. That would give him a good start. If he was super cautious, there may be enough remaining ignorant casinos to allow him to make a fairly decent living playing blackjack without being totally blackballed.

It was shortly before lunch he suddenly broke free from his tenacious bout of self-incertitude. It was like he had been in some kind of trance. All of a sudden, he couldn't believe he had been considering the possibility of giving up this late in the game. His master plan hadn't anticipated something like this might happen. If he had it to do again, he would have definitely included a segment to better prepare him for such a self-doubt contingency.

He would be ready for the next nightmare if it came again. It wouldn't take him half the day to question his grit and unassailable determination. He was 100% back to come what may. He had successfully proceeded too far to get weak knees now. The hardest part was over. The chance of being caught had diminished significantly. In some ways, his brief period of doubt had actually hardened his resolve. It was time to to get back to work with even more vigor and positive determination.

Back in the saddle, SAs Cook and Lytle were licking their wounds. Their most promising investigative gambit had fallen through the cracks. Although the failure of their last ditch effort to bargain Mandy hadn't come as a big surprise, it was still a disappointment leaving them demoralized and squarely back at ground zero.

With dozens of surveillance attempts having proved totally unproductive and the scant chance of catching their prey off guard in another undercover attempt, they rationalized time was still their ally and they could afford to wait to pounce once Sam finally decided to spend the money. Patience would surely prevail in the end. It had to.

TWENTY-EIGHT

Part of Sam's master plan included the use of a small blue spiral notebook for the purpose of keeping track of exactly what had occurred in each of the casinos where the stolen funds had been laundered. Since his plan required returning to each of the approximately 150 casinos as many as four times, it was imperative he recall the details of each casino encounter.

He divided the notebook into six narrow columns including "Date", "Name", "Event", "Time", "Worker(s)" and "Costume". The date was one of four times he had appeared at each of the casinos. The name was an abbreviation for the casino. He used a short notation for the event which showed "pc" for when he purchased chips and played blackjack and "cc" for when he cashed in the chips. The time showed when he entered and left. The worker column showed the last name of the casino employees he had dealt with including dealers and cashiers. The last column disclosed a number from one to four, each representing one of four different costumes.

If the laundering proceeded on schedule, there should be four entries for each of the casinos. The first would reflect the purchase of $5,000 worth of chips. The second would be for the purchase of an additional $5,000. The third would record cashing in approximately $5,000 of chips and the fourth entry for cashing in the remaining $5,000. It was approximate because cashing in the chips would include any chips Sam had won in addition to those he purchased. Of course, there was always a chance he might lose some chips, but he didn't consider that a likely outcome. As it eventually turned out, his cockiness was justified.

The importance of assiduously maintaining the record couldn't be overemphasized in his way of thinking. Amplifying the chance of success involved never entering the same casino with the same costume and never dealing with the same casino employee more than once. He had decided on the four costumes that were the most realistic and least likely to cause a suspicious glance. As far as the employees, he tried to make sure as far as practicable to pick alternate shifts when different employees were on duty.

The notebook was stored in the hidden compartment under the front passenger seat of the Corolla. Concealing its existence was the prudent step to take. There was no use in taking any unnecessary chances that might allow the FBI to prematurely suspect what he may be up to, even though the process was now far along enough that no ties to the stolen funds could be proven beyond a reasonable doubt. Sam felt confident there would be insufficient evidence to convince any potential jury his purchase of chips hadn't originated from his legal winnings.

It was the second week in October and he was well into the second phase of converting chips to casino checks. In less than five months, way quicker than he at first estimated, the original stolen cash had been assimilated into the momentary system with no chance of being traced back to its source. Just as with the initial purchase of chips, his carefully conceived plan called for reappearing at 15 of the 150 casinos per day. Each stop would take no more than a few minutes to appear at the cashier cage and cash in $5,000 plus worth of fifty and hundred dollar chips for a check of equal value payable to his true name.

He would then return approximately 10 days later to the same casinos to similarly convert another $5,000 plus while appearing to a different cashier and wearing a different costume. Should management become suspicious after it was somehow, although unlikely, determined the same basic transaction had occurred with checks of essentially equal amounts being issued to the same person, a red flag could be conceivably raised to be on the lookout for any similar future transactions. It would be a useless precaution since it wasn't going to happen again. Passing the information on to law enforcement as possible money laundering was improbable because of the relatively minimalist activity involved for any one casino.

"Hi, I've got some chips I'd like to cash in." Sam had approached the cashier's cage at Sam's Town east of the Strip. The woman at the cage had a badge identifying her with the last name of Bradley. She showed no indication of suspecting that he was in disguise mode. Had there been any question, he would have made some kind of excuse and returned at a later time when another employee was working the cage.

"How much we talking about," Bradley questioned.

"I'm guessing there's about five thousand bucks in 50 and 100 dollar chips," Sam replied as if he did this all the time.

"Do you have a club card?"

"No, I never signed up. I've never really been interested in going that route. Is that a problem?

"Not really," Bradley answered. "Although, you might be making a mistake. That way you would have a record to establish losses and help reduce your taxes. But, it's your choice."

"I'll have to think about that. Wouldn't do that much good now with the tax year almost over."

"How do you want your money? Cash or check?"

"Check. If you don't mind," he responded. "Don't like carrying that much cash around."

It took a couple more minutes until he exited Sam's Town with a check in the amount of $6, 350 payable to his true name with no one apparently any wiser as to the part they had just played in his master plan. He quickly filled out the details in his notebook and proceeded on to the next casino to repeat the same procedure. So far, so good. It was like taking candy from a baby.

TWENTY-NINE

The workload of the St. George Resident Agency had increased considerably over the past year. Both SAs now had caseloads in excess 30 investigations each. Some of them were one shot leads from other offices, but they both had numerous cases identified as "office of origin" which meant they were ultimately responsible for the total investigative effort required to bring the cases to a logical conclusion.

SA Cook had one especially complicated white collar case involving a pyramid scheme by a self-promoted con man who had defrauded dozens of trusting investors scattered all over the Intermountain West. By the time he got the case, customers at the bottom of the pyramid had lost in excess of half a million dollars. It was imperative the case be indicted at the earliest possible date to avoid even greater losses. Investors were in denial and the best way to convince them they had been swindled and prevent even more victims was to initiate a speedy arrest.

That meant he was spending the majority of his workday interviewing local victims, sending out leads to other offices, and digging through volumes of investor agreements and related correspondence to identify counts that could be included in an indictment. The rest of his case load was falling behind and he was still being assigned new priority assignments every week.

The more inexperienced of the two, SA Lytle was also up to his neck in alligators. His most pressing case involved an extortion already indicted and about ready to go to trial. Although there was talk of placing a U.S. District Judge in St. George, it hadn't happened yet and that meant it would be tried in Salt Lake City 300 miles away. To make matters worse, AUSA Samuelson had been placed on extended medical leave. Tony therefore had to work with an unfamiliar AUSA stationed at the federal courthouse in Salt Lake.

That meant being required to make numerous trips back and forth between the two cities to liaison with the new AUSA including sitting in with witnesses who were being prepped for the testimony they would be giving in court. Add the necessity of trying to keep on top of all his other case load assignments and it was difficult to distinguish which one of the two agents was the most overworked.

What was needed was to add at least one and preferably two more agents to the St. George RA. The problem was that most likely wasn't going to be happening anytime in the foreseeable future. With the normal number of forced retirements at age fifty-five continuing at its normal pace, there had been a decreasing number of new agent classes at the Quantico, Virginia training center. Combine that with an increase in overall caseload and all the offices were starting to feel the crunch. There just weren't enough new agents to go around.

FBI management blamed the Republicans in Congress who seemed obsessed with solving the deficit crisis by cutting federal employment as much as possible. They seemed to think public employees (both federal and state) were a drain on society. The more you could cut them back, the better. They were unwilling to increase taxes on the super-rich through closing unfair tax loopholes no one but the rich could take advantage of. Cutting back tax incentives for large corporations that were making obscene profits was non-negotiable. Their only acceptable solution was to cut federal spending.

To make matters worse, America was just coming out of a major financial meltdown that many attributed to an unnecessary war in Iraq and financial shenanigans by Wall Street corporations involved in the real estate industry. Instead of increasing taxes to pay for the war, President Bush enacted a decrease in the tax rate. Unemployment was still too high in many parts of America and President Obama and Democrats were pushing first for job stimulus measures to be followed by more serious deficit reduction further into the recovery. Republicans never saw a stimulus package they could stomach.

The net effect on the Sam Scam couldn't have been more fortuitous had he been capable of including it as part of his master plan. Although he didn't let down his guard in the least, the reality of the current situation was he could have been considerably less cautious. The chance of him being caught by the FBI in the act of engaging in his carefully orchestrated money laundering strategy had for the last couple of months been minimal at best.

***

"I just finished reviewing Donahue's bank records for September. The only thing that seems to stand out is he's withdrawing more cash while increasing the amount he owes on his credit cards. There's no way to know for sure how it's being spent. He's making only the minimum amount of monthly payments. He's still got a ways to go before he maxes out his lines of credit, but seems on a consistent path to eventually have that happen." SA Cook was sharing with Tony the results of what limited investigation he had been able to deal with on the Sam Scam.

"Doesn't sound like he's spending much of the loot, does it?, Tony lamented. "Any indication he's rented anymore cars? That jeep has always seemed a little suspicious to me."

"If he has, he hasn't used any of his credit cards. He's not going to be able to rent a car without furnishing one. I suppose he could have somehow gotten hold of a false driver's license, but that would be the only way. I couldn't make anything out of the mileage with the jeep. He could have gone anywhere. I've got a stop with all the rental companies in Vegas if he tries again, but so far nothing."

'It seems he's spending an inordinate amount of time in Las Vegas playing the blackjack tables," Tony offered. "You have to believe he's suffered some significant loses by now. I just can't believe he's not going to have to dig into his booty before long."

"Well, that's what we've got to keep hoping will happen. Neither of us has much time to devote to him now. I just need to keep an eye on his financial stuff right now and hope for a break. All his spending so far appears based on legitimate sources of income. As far as the blackjack angle goes, what little contact I've been able to make with the dealers and cocktail waitresses indicates he plays a mean game and is actually winning a significant portion of the time. Other than that, he's evidently quite a lady's man. He's one of those lucky guys with the kind of looks causing even the most attractive of women to swoon without much effort. Lucky fellow."

"Yeah, that would be nice. I unfortunately have never encountered that kind of adoration from the gentler sex. Any limited success I've garnered has been a result of my extraordinary intelligence and sense of humor," Tony responded in an attempt to lighten the atmosphere. "Have you thought about making another effort to tempt any of his new sweeties with the reward money?"

"Actually, I have thought about it. I know we weren't too successful the last time, but it was the best thing we had going there for a while. There certainly seems enough more of them to potentially choose from, but finding time to attempt to develop any new informants is the problem now."

THIRTY

Following his affair with Mandy, Sam was back to his previous practice of minimal involvement with numerous different stimulating beauties, most of whom worked at the casinos he patronized. Spending more than a night or two with any of them was unusual. There was certainly no desire on his part to once again get involved in any kind of a serious relationship. Nevertheless, his physical appearance and engaging personality enabled him to attract the best Vegas had to offer, and he saw no reason not to take advantage of those ever-present opportunities.

His facial feature was eerily similar to that of John F. Kennedy Jr., son of the former President, who died when his Piper Saratoga light aircraft plunged into the Connecticut coastline in the summer of 1999. Some guys are just born with the DNA that attracts women. Both he and Kennedy had that unique ability to turn the heads of even the most attractive of the female species who normally wouldn't consider openly exposing their attraction in that fashion.

When he entered a casino, it wasn't long before the cocktail waitresses were punching each other in the arm and whispering about that handsome hunk who had just started playing at this or that blackjack table. For the lucky one who got to offer him refreshments and engage in small talk, the rest of her co-workers frequently berated her with a barrage of suggestive sexual innuendo concerning about what it would be like to engage him in this or that compromising situation.

What drove women even further over the edge was once treated to his sexual prowess, they wanted more. He had done his homework over the years and was well educated in what it took to satisfy even the most orgasmic challenged. Not only was he more amply endowed than the average male, but that provided only part of his copulatory arsenal. First, he took his time with numerous expert erotic techniques guaranteed to leave his totally engrossed partners begging for his final ravishment.

He enjoyed his sexual conquests as much as did his numerous willing partners. Still, he wanted more than that in any permanent relationship. Mandy had temporarily filled that need but what a disaster it had turned out to be. She had been intelligent and they shared the same interests. He felt totally at ease in her presence. Up until the end, he loved her sense of humor. But now, he was more cautious than ever. He wondered if he would ever allow himself to be so completely enamored again.

He made it a practice to fully inform his willing conquests his interest in a tryst, although sincere and desired, was meant to be limited in duration. He wanted them to know that up-front and not be offended when that was all it turned out to be. It was just his life was preoccupied with other matters and there was currently no room in it for any kind of extended relationship. Most women accepted those terms going in and many said they felt the very same way. Several said they were only interested in temporarily experiencing what others had been touting as having been a totally satisfying intimate encounter.

Not every woman, however, took his warning to heart. Every once in a while, someone seemed to forget she had been forewarned and had agreed to limited participation. One in particular, Judith, didn't take it at all well when Sam reminded her their minimalist engagement had never been intended to extend past a couple of nights. Being an extremely attractive cocktail waitress and not used to being rebuffed by a man, she first used every female wile she had ever learned to make her an exception to the rule. When it didn't work, she became irate and cussed him up one side and down the other in a way that would have made even a drunken sailor blush.

Although it wouldn't have made any difference in him quickly distancing himself from this unpleasant damsel in distress, there had been another reason for not wanting to deal with her any further that hadn't surfaced until they were actively engaged. That was her revelation she periodically socialized with Mandy and her roommate. Had he known that, he would have never agreed to add her to his list of conquests. Who knows what information Mandy may have shared? He would be careful in the future to eliminate any friends of Mandy or Julie from his list of potential playmates.

He made it a practice never to date women while in disguise mode. That wouldn't have worked out if, for example, his fake nose came loose while they were intimately cavorting. In addition, it was important to create witnesses who could later testify to his card playing prowess. Thus, he only fooled around when he intentionally wanted to be remembered in his true identity.

The autumn leaves had fallen and the first snowfall of the year was being forecast for St. George. With the exception of the final ten casinos, all the chips had been successfully converted to checks. His extraordinarily ambitious venture was nearing the end. He was actually a couple of weeks ahead of where he had planned to be at this point in time. After converting the remaining chips, the only thing left was to deposit the checks.

His master plan required the deposits be made before the end of the calendar year for tax reasons. But, he also didn't want those deposits to be made until as close to the end of December as possible. He had selected 12 different banks in the Las Vegas area with each receiving multiple deposits over a period of several days. With three deposits per bank, that would result in no single deposit of more than $50,000.

Because he was now ahead of schedule, he decided to devote some extra time in reinforcing his reputation as a blackjack player extraordinaire. With no disguises and making a concerted effort to embed his true identity in the minds of the casino employees, he used every card skill in his arsenal to run off a string of winnings leaving little doubt he was a player to be reckoned with and closely watched.

He made sure to choose the casinos that would most likely be visited by the FBI to determine the true extent of his card playing skills. He selected the ones he knew he had been previously followed into by the FBI. Most of them already contained witnesses, including his numerous sexual conquests, who would vouch for his expertise. These last forays would undoubtedly add even more fuel to his stellar reputation.

After a couple of weeks of being watched from the cameras on high, he was finally distinguished as a card counter at the Excalibur on the Strip. He was politely taken aside and informed he would no longer be welcome at the blackjack tables. Little did these enforcers realize they had just played a key role in the master design. His tarnished standing at this late stage of the game was exactly what he had hoped to achieve. Evidence to support his ability to win big was just what the doctor ordered.

THIRTY-ONE

It was what had become a normal Monday morning with SAs Cook and Lytle busily organizing the leads from other offices having arrived over the weekend. Nothing terribly urgent, but several new brief assignments would require coverage before the end of the week. It was December 2 and Steve had celebrated his 30th birthday the day before. His wife had wanted to stage a party with black balloons etc., but he had talked her out of it. Instead, he was able to spend a relaxing Sunday answering multiple calls from family and well-wishers scattered over several states.

Tony answered the phone and placed it on hold a little after 10am. He shouted over to Steve who was busy sending a fax. "There's a lady on the phone who says she has information about the armored car robbery. Figured you'd want to talk to her since you've got the ticket."

"Thanks a lot!" Steve snidely replied. "Wouldn't want you to disrespect my authority by helping out a little. Just kidding, bud. Switch her over."

"Special Agent Cook. Who am I talking to and how can I help you?"

"My name is Judith Reynolds. I've only got a minute. I'm on break. I work at Bally's in Las Vegas. I'm a cocktail waitress."

"What can I do for you, Judith?"

"I'm a friend of Mandy Diaz. She told me about the reward being offered for the armored car robbery. Is that still available?"

"Yes it is. Do you think you might qualify?"

"I'm hoping I might." she responded. "I've been on a couple of dates with Sam Donahue. I think you might be interested in what he has confided in me. He's hinted he's sitting on a pot full of money nobody but he knows about."

Although wary about this new development, Steve suggested, "I'm busy right now, but I'd like to sit down with you in person at your earliest convenience. It would help if you could come to our office in St. George. Would that be possible? How about later this afternoon or tomorrow morning?"

"I guess I could do that. I'm not working tomorrow in the morning. I could be there about nine, but I'd have to leave no later than eleven"

"Sounds good. Do you know where our office is located?"

"Yes, I've got the address in the phone book and GPS."

"Ok then, see you in the morning. Just ring the bell and we'll buzz you in."

After filling Tony in on the gist of the conversation, Steve asked if he could join him in the interview so there would be two of them to witness what she had to say.

Tony readily agreed, but added his skepticism about the value of talking to her. "It's hard for me to believe she's telling the truth. What's the chance of Sam the scam man sharing something with her that's potentially damaging when he didn't come close to it with Mandy? Sounds fishy to me."

"I agree, but what've we got to lose? She's coming here and it shouldn't take long to see what she has to offer. It's difficult to imagine him trusting another girlfriend after being set up by Mandy, but who can tell for sure. Maybe he was too drunk to realize what he said. Who knows whatever other reason there may be for catching him off guard? I can't believe he's not going to mess up somewhere down the road. No one's that perfect. This may be one of those rare lapses of caution. We're in no position to disregard even the most unlikely of possibilities."

The chips were all cashed in. Although Sam had been confident his carefully planned scheme had a good chance of succeeding, he continued to be somewhat surprised and elated it had thus far proceeded so smoothly. There was no longer any need for his rental house or storage shed. He informed the landlord via mail that November would be his last month. He used a pay phone to tell the operator of the storage shed the same thing. He mailed the final payment to both with hard to discover cashier checks drawn on banks unrelated to his normal financial activities.

He paid cash to rent a delivery truck for two hours from Home Depot to empty the shed. He trashed the desk and bookcases at the local dump. He planned to transfer title to the car he bought in New Mexico to a local Las Vegas charity. Although it wouldn't present that much of a problem to explain the existence of the car come tax time, he didn't plan to claim the value as a deduction. Why highlight anything that could even slightly point to part of his scheme. It wasn't like he was going to need a financial deduction for that small amount from the IRS.

If need be, he would explain the purchase of the car as nothing more than an effort to make it more difficult for the FBI to follow him. He was tired of having his privacy continually violated. If it ever came to it, the shenanigans at the 150 casinos with disguises etc. could be easily explained as an effort not to be expelled for counting cards. Nothing illegal about that. Any half intelligent card counter might do the same. In reality, he was confident none of these explanations would ever be required in any future court proceeding. It appeared the FBI's interest in him had slacked off considerably.

The depositing of casino checks would commence in the next couple of weeks. In the meantime, he had chosen one of the banks selected and rented a safe deposit box to temporarily store all 300 checks. Copies of the checks would come to the attention of the FBI after he filed his tax return the following April. They would have no doubt they represented the washed proceeds of the stolen funds, but they were going to have one heck of time trying to prove it. Actually, the way he had it figured, there was no way now they could possibly prove the deposits weren't the result of totally legal gambling winnings.

THIRTY-TWO

SA Cook looked at the color monitor linked to the hall camera revealing visitors who rang the bell on the third floor of their modest FBI office in St. George. His watch displayed exactly 8:50 am. Having arrived ahead of schedule, an exceptionally attractive female waited for a response. *What a lady's man,* Steve marveled to himself. He was forced to envy his irritating nemeses' ability to attract the sexiest Las Vegas had to offer. He hit the buzzer simultaneously unlocking the latch to allow entrance to a small waiting room leading into a single office space with two desks at opposite ends. Both he and Tony arose to welcome the curvaceous potential informer.

"I hope it's no problem I'm a little early," Judith Reynolds apologized. "It didn't take me as long as I thought to get here and I wanted to make sure we had enough time. I need to get back as soon as possible to start my afternoon shift."

"No problem at all," Steve graciously responded. "We're just having some coffee waiting for your arrival. Can I get you a cup? How do you like it?"

"Yes, that would be nice. A little cream and one packet of sugar, please."

After handing her some Folgers instant in a Styrofoam cup, he led her to a hard back wood chair across from his desk and informed her Tony would be sitting in on the interview.

"We really appreciate you coming over today." As was the normal course, Steve would conduct the interview until the very end when he would offer Tony the opportunity to inquire into any unanswered questions he still had. "I'd like to start by getting a little identifying information."

She was twenty-seven, single and lived alone in an apartment a short distance from where she had full-time employment as a cocktail waitress at Bally's. She had been working there for slightly over two years. She provided her social security number and denied any criminal history. She allowed Tony to take a picture of her and make a copy of her driver's license for the file.

"I think its best we get right to the point so as not to infringe on your tight schedule," Steve continued. "Tell us exactly the circumstances and what Sam told you that might help you qualify for the reward. But, before you start, let me remind you the reward is only given out if it ends up being determined your information leads to a successful prosecution. Specifically, if he was to be acquitted, there would be no reward. Do you understand that?"

"I do now," Judy somewhat glumly confirmed. "I've dated Sam twice. It was on the second date, the day after this past Thanksgiving when we were at my apartment and had just enjoyed each other's company if you know what I mean. We were both still a little tipsy after enjoying some exotic cocktails I'm known for concocting. I may have overdone it a little with the gin. Anyway, we somehow got on the topic of living expenses and how hard it was to make ends meet these days. Then, out of the blue, he blurted he had a stash of money nobody knew about and financial security was going to be the least of his worries."

"I need you to tell me exactly what he said about the money." Steve pressed. "Did he mention an amount? I need his exact words the best you can remember."

"That's pretty much exactly what he said." There was no ambiguity about what he meant. We changed topics and didn't talk about it any further. He never mentioned an amount of money, but I got the impression from his tone of voice it was considerable. Is that going to be helpful in your investigation?"

"It might be." Steve didn't want to sound too discouraging just in case this new potential witness may be of some worth. The reality is it would take a lot more than she said- he said to make a case. "The problem is it's just your word against his at this point in time. What would you say about meeting up with him again and trying to get him to repeat the same thing once more while the conversation was being recorded?"

"That's not going to happen." Judy sounded a little discouraged. "He made it quite clear he wasn't interested in dating me anymore. The conversation got ugly and I can't imagine even the slightest possibility we might get back together. Surely, what he said has got to count for something."

"Most likely not quite enough, but we'll run it past the prosecutor just in case to see what he thinks. But, I'm almost certain he's going to respond we need more to confirm what you're saying actually happened. It's not I don't believe you. The problem is a good defense attorney would most likely be successful in convincing a jury you were only interested in the reward money. That's just the way it is. Are you sure there isn't something else we can use to support your story?"

"Not really, that's about it," Judy replied in an increasingly negative tone of voice.

"Don't take what I'm about to say wrong, Judith," Steve warned. "But, in interviews like this, I'm required to inform you that you can be prosecuted for providing false information to the FBI. That means we would want you to submit to a polygraph examination. I hope you wouldn't have a problem with that to help confirm your honesty. You wouldn't have a problem with that would you?"

Judy's mind was now racing wildly. What had she got herself into? There was no doubt she was lying and the polygraph would most likely confirm her deception. All of a sudden, she decided she needed to extradite herself out of this mess before it was too late. All she could think to do was to profess disgust to somewhat salve her ego and immediately disengage herself from this botched attempt at getting rich quick.

"To hell with you," she bellowed. "I'm not taking any damned polygraph test. If you can't take me at my word, than you can take your truth machine and stick it up where the sun doesn't shine. Forget I ever came in here. Forget I ever said anything. As far as I'm concerned, I'm through trying to cooperate with you and I refuse to testify about anything." With that, she rose in a show of indignation and left the office in a huff.

Of course, Steve would still write up a record of interview and include in it everything that had occurred and been said. A prosecutor could still require her to testify as an uncooperative witness, but that wasn't going to happen. She would be pretty much worthless as a credible witness. It would take confirming evidence to support her story and that slight possibility appeared essentially nonexistent.

What he hadn't explained in his threat of a polygraph examination was the results of such a test couldn't be used against her to convict her of lying. Even if she flunked, the legal system had long ago concluded the results of such tests weren't reliable enough to be used in court. The polygraph was mostly an investigative tool attempting to get subjects and witnesses to come clean.

In this case, the threat was enough to confirm she had been nothing but a gold digger. They had suspected that all along and therefore weren't all that disappointed. They were back were they had left off before she called. They had wasted only a little over an hour to confirm their doubt.

THIRTY-THREE

The checks were all deposited. It was three days after Christmas with several days to spare to ensure all the alleged gambling winnings would reflect 2015 earnings. There had been only a minor glitch when one of the tellers showed a little too much interest while depositing checks from the Venetian. She seemed overly curious in exactly what he had done to win the money. No big deal, but Sam preferred tellers who showed little interest in their customer's activities. He closed the account the next morning and deposited the amount withdrawn in another bank with a less inquisitive teller.

The massive deposits in his true name would hopefully not become known to the FBI until sometime after he filed his return which he planned to hold off until the deadline in April. His reasoning was he wanted to continue to build on his reputation as an expert blackjack player before the shit hit the fan. The more he proved he could win large sums by playing cards, the harder it was going to be to prove the source of the deposits weren't legally earned. If the FBI became aware of his deposit history earlier, his previous, although somewhat limited, stellar play would still afford him a difficult to refute vindication. Still, it didn't hurt to beef up that defense even more with several more months of impressive winnings.

It's been estimated the odds of winning a hand for an average blackjack player is approximately once out of every 2.2 attempts. He figured it was more like one out of 3 for him, but for losing instead of winning. A persistent concern, however, was he couldn't continue to win like that without security eventually determining his fortunate play relied on card counting. If and when such an eventuality finally materialized, his welcome at that particular casino would in all likelihood be withdrawn, sometimes politely and other times not so much.

Christmas Day had been a non-event in his life this year. In years past, the obligatory office party had at least provided him a piece of the holiday spirit. With his bevy of potential one night stands spending the holiday with their families, he had spent the day alone at his apartment in St. George. With no family or long term friends to speak of, he hadn't been invited over anywhere for Christmas dinner. He didn't see that as a concern. The fewer the people sentimentally tied to him, the less the chance of his master plan being foiled.

New Year's Eve in Las Vegas would be different. It was one of the hottest spots to celebrate the coming of 2016. Already, there were several beauties vying for their pick as his date. He'd make his ultimate choice in the next day or two. This would be a landmark year to celebrate for sure. He'd banked the entire amount of his theft plus more from superior card playing skills to do with what he pleased. The threat of arrest and incarceration was in his mind no longer a threat at all. His planning had been too meticulous and had proceeded better than he could have hoped to be derailed now. His fortune was now reasonably secure. His master plan had so far resulted in a dazzling success.

It was the second week in January of 2016 and SA Cook had made the 300 mile trip from St. George to Salt Lake to conduct a file review with his immediate supervisor. This was different than the previous ones in that his former boss had been transferred out of the division and he was being grilled by his new chief, Tim Forester, for the first time. This would be the first time Forester had a chance to go over each case assigned to the St. George RA to make sure the Senior Resident Agent was handling each investigative assignment in the most comprehensive and efficient manner possible.

"It's obvious you and your partner are struggling with a challenging workload down there," Forester sympathetically acknowledged. "What bothers me, though, is the case assigned to you involving the armored car theft doesn't appear to be getting the attention it deserves. There seems to be little doubt this fellow Donahue has stolen the money. Normally, when you know who committed a crime, it should make it easier to wrap a case up. It's been way too long now and we don't seem to be any closer than the first day you took his signed statement."

"I know boss. The guy has been a tough nut to crack. There's no doubt about that. We tailed him up to the point it became apparent the chance of success in using that particular strategy didn't seem to justify the continued expenditure of manpower. We've tried using our crack surveillance teams more than once. Las Vegas is a nightmare. Following him once he gets into the downtown area has gotten us nowhere. We've interviewed everyone we can think of and nothing. We've taped his conversations with a promising informant. We conducted an undercover sting. None of our normal techniques have worked. His financial affairs haven't as of yet disclosed any indication of the theft."

"Maybe it's time we tried another full court press," Forester suggested. "He probably figures we have given up following him. That means he might have become a little less cautious. If we could follow his every move for a week, I can't believe we wouldn't be able to observe something, no matter how small, that would somehow tie him into the stolen money. What would you think about giving it another concerted push? I could assign a couple of Salt Lake agents to handle some of your leads to free you and Tony up for a short period."

"That's fine with me. It would obviously mean bringing in the Salt Lake surveillance team again. That didn't work before. I hate to waste their valuable time if it doesn't pan out once more. I may become their worst enemy."

"You let me worry about that. I'll make sure they know it was entirely my idea. We'll do it a little different this time. This time he won't be able to elude us. I'll arrange for the Las Vegas team to join up with ours. Not only that, I'll devote five more agents from Salt Lake to be detailed to the effort for a week. Maybe, we can even get some extra agents from Las Vegas to join in. He won't be able to make a move without us knowing his every step. We'll give it a week and see what happens. What do you say?"

"Sounds great," Steve's enthusiasm was suddenly on the upturn. This was definitely an offer too good to refuse. "Let's do it."

THIRTY-FOUR

Finally, everything was in place to follow Sam's every move for the next five days, 24 hrs./day, from Tuesday morning through however late he stayed up on the following Saturday. It was the middle of February. It had taken a month to free up and coordinate the surveillance teams from Salt Lake and Las Vegas. It hadn't been easy.

Both specialized Salt Lake and Las Vegas surveillance team leaders had argued more productive use of their talents. In the end, both Special Agents in Charge had finally agreed to give it one more try by using the best resources each had to offer. That included not only both surveillance teams, but five additional agents from each division and the single engine plane assigned to Vegas.

Sam had months ago decided he was no longer being constantly followed. That didn't mean he hadn't still been somewhat cautious by assuming he was being tailed wherever he went. It was just he had stopped obsessing in his rear view mirror and continually glancing up into the wild blue yonder. Now, it really didn't matter all that much. He no longer had to worry about being seen in his discarded second car or being followed to his former Vegas apartment and storage shed.

Discovering his numerous bank accounts would accelerate the discovery of his fortune, but no real harm would result. It would just move up the clock a bit. By May, at the latest, the FBI would be fully aware of his revised net worth having moved in a startlingly and suspicious upward direction. He had tried to limit his visits to the numerous banks to help preclude a premature disclosure of his financial dealings. So far, he didn't think he had been followed, but there was no way to know for sure since he was no longer hyper-careful about his travel as had previously been his practice.

By the end of January, he had consolidated his funds at one bank. He had then transferred 3/4ths of his money to an off-shore account in the Cayman Islands. That would leave enough to pay his taxes and pay off his credit card debt while still maintaining sufficient funds to live comfortably for the foreseeable future. He made the transfer just in case the government decided to start impounding his accounts. He didn't see any way they could legally do that, but why take a chance. The overseas account was much safer from any such attempted seizure.

The fully augmented surveillance team was superbly ensconced by 5am on Tuesday morning. A team of five cars were strategically stationed to follow Sam when he left his apartment in St. George. He had been put to bed there the night before. These particular agents were highly trained professionals in the art of following without being detected.

It would be rare if Sam picked them up even if he was being exceptionally cautious, which he wasn't. The Las Vegas plane was sitting on the tarmac of the St. George airport and ready to lift into the clear blue yonder at a moment's notice. The weather was mild with a forecasted high of 65 degrees.

Tuesday ended up a disappointing bust with the vast majority of topnotch eagle eyes sitting on their collective butt cheeks with nothing to do. That was because Sam went straight to the golf course in St George at around 9am where he spent the rest of the morning and part of the afternoon practicing on the driving range and following up with an 18 hole round. He had joined a man and wife to make a threesome. It was later determined by SA Lytle he most likely didn't know the couple before he randomly joined up with them. He paid using one of his known credit cards.

The pro at the course later advised he was an above-average golfer. Those who played with him vouched for his ability noting his drives more often than not landed on the fairway averaging over 200 yards. His short game was nothing to sneer at either. The PGA showed a handicap of sixteen for 18 holes. He was pretty much of a loner who seldom seemed to have plans to play with anyone in particular. There were a couple of attractive single women who he temporarily teamed up with but those associations appeared to end up short-lived.

After his round of golf, he proceeded to a local Chili's restaurant where he was observed eating alone while partaking in a late lunch consisting of a hamburger and draft beer. He then returned to his apartment where he remained until mid-morning on Wednesday. Steve and Tony were becoming nervous. They felt responsible for tying up such a significant contingent of prime manpower. They could only hope the rest of the week turned out to be more productive. Otherwise, they could anticipate the criticism and embarrassment from their fellow agents that would inevitably follow.

From Wednesday on, the surveillance picked up with most of the agents fully participating in attempting to catch their target doing something to expose his embezzling ways. Thank God, both Steve and Tony breathed a sigh he hadn't chosen this entire week to stay close at home. Instead, he headed straight for Las Vegas and wouldn't return home until the following Sunday morning.

The first two nights, he was given a comp for a luxury suite atop the Luxor on the south end of the Strip. Recently, exposing his true self with no costuming involved, he had made sure those tasked with handing out such favors were made aware of his regular play at the blackjack tables. He had made sure not to win too much more than he lost, but he also won big on two occasions to prove to anyone inquiring he had the capability of being an exceptional player.

Although being put up at the Luxor, he moved around to several other casinos during the two day stay. This challenged the entire surveillance team to keep up with his goings and comings. Much of his movement was on foot up and down the Strip. No one ever lost sight of him but came close on a couple of occasions. His play was similar to what he was trying to promote at the Luxor. Anyone inquiring about his competence would give him high marks.

He was a uncharacteristically careless and won a little too much at Imperial Palace. He was accused of card counting after accumulating chips in excess of $10,000 over a period a little less than an hour. He was firmly escorted out of the casino and sternly warned not to return. He could only hope that management didn't share its concern with other casinos in the area.

Actually, unknown to him, things couldn't have worked out better as a follow up interview by SA Cook found out the details of the suspicion behind the ouster not long after the surveillance team had first observed the entire incident. Alas, more proof about how he could have won the money instead of stolen it. Cool!

THIRTY-FIVE

The last two days of the massive surveillance provided a new wrinkle. Close to 10am on Thursday morning, Sam was observed meeting a scintillating brunette in the lobby of the Luxor just prior to checking out. Sporting long shapely tanned legs and a mini skirt, she definitely hadn't been seen with him the night before. Nobody noticed how she'd arrived. She had a small designer suitcase placed in the trunk of Sam's car along with his stuff as they exited the Luxor parking lot.

It was later determined the stunner was 26 year old Brenda Cushing, a concierge at New York New York just up the street. She'd been recently divorced and was considered by those later interviewed to be a rising star in the gaming industry. It may not help much should her superiors somehow learn she had been contacted by the FBI about associating with a gambler suspected of nefarious conduct. When initially questioned at work by SA Cook the Sunday following the end of the surveillance, she acknowledged meeting Sam for the first time two weeks previous when they agreed on a date to travel together on a pleasure trip to Reno.

Both spent Thursday and Friday nights at the Summit at Grand Sierra Resort & Casino on Second St. in Reno. There wasn't a move either made outside their room that wasn't observed by the crack surveillance team. It immediately became clear this wasn't his first trip to the casino. It was obvious management and many of the employees, particularly around the blackjack tables, had comped him before.

That was verified when later determined he had been provided free of charge access to the Grand II Suite with all its luxurious amenities including custom leather furniture, spa showers and flat screen televisions. Free meal tickets at the best restaurant in the resort were also furnished. Lucky agents who discreetly covered the entire casino amenities were treated to the bikini clad Brenda as they lounged around the large outdoor pool complete with beach sand and cabanas. What a body! Sam really knew how to pick his lady friends.

The casino expected him to spend considerable time at the blackjack tables. That's what he had done several times previously and why they were providing him complimentary services now. He didn't disappoint. Agents observed him at the tables for just over a total of ten hours during the two day period. Brenda stood by him some of the time, but she mostly treated herself to time at the spa and health club where she worked out, received two different exotic massages and had her hair done, all of which it was later determined she paid for with her own Visa card.

Sam signed up for a player card. Because he no longer needed to hide the source of his funds, the card was the way to go since it compiled the amount he spent on chips as well as what he got back when he cashed in. The yearly computer summary freely provided by the casino would furnish the proof he needed to ensure he was only taxed on his net winnings.

For the first 6 hours or so, he played the tables just like before by winning just enough so as not to create suspicion of card counting. This time, however, he spent the last four hours displaying his full expertise. He walked away with a net profit of $15,000. Although he was talented, this was an extraordinary streak of luck. Normally he could count on winning more than he lost, but he hadn't ever won this much before at a single sitting.

He wasn't sure how management would take it. Since he didn't plan on returning to this particular resort again, he really didn't care. It wouldn't surprise him if he was placed on the card counting watch list. Whether further gratis amenities may have been offered in the future was problematic. Such perks are usually reserved for compulsive net losers.

One potential benefit was the possibility the FBI would eventually discover his superlative play on this particular occasion. That certainly wouldn't aid their effort to help prove he couldn't in a million years have won enough playing blackjack to account for his newfound wealth. Little did he know that was what ended up happening and was exactly the type of evidence any potential prosecutor would dread being required to share with a defense attorney. The master plan didn't mandate this specific lucky streak, but it sure didn't hurt.

Up until she told him about her interview after their trip, he had no idea they had been followed. No matter. Nothing they had done or anything he had talked about with her could provide even a scintilla of evidence to tie him in any way to the embezzlement. That had been their last date. As was becoming the norm with his dating modus operandi, they had both agreed beforehand their brief excursion to Reno would be the extent of their relationship together. Neither was interested in anything more than a single fling.

Although not unexpected, the mood in the St. George FBI office Monday morning following the disappointing surveillance was sullen to say the least.

"I was afraid this would happen," Steve lamented to his equally dispirited partner. "I wished I had talked Forester out of it. Not only are we not any closer to solving anything, but what little credibility we had with the Las Vegas division and our own surveillance team has dissolved like sugar in a hot cup of coffee. I hate to think about trying to get either to help us when another case comes along that screams for their assistance. We've pretty much used up the last of our collateral."

"I don't think it's all that bad." Tony hadn't seen Steve this emotionally drained before and tried to bring him back to more of a sense of equilibrium. "These guys get paid the same regardless. They've been on enough unsuccessful operations not to let it bother them that much. We're the same way. Failure is part of the job. You just go on to the next assignment and hope it works out better. One thing for sure, though, if there was ever any doubt before, there shouldn't be any now. He doesn't appear ready to play his hand at the moment. Following him isn't going to help. We're going to have to wait until he starts to spend the booty.

"I know you're right," Steve reluctantly admitted. "Damn Sam! I just wish he would get started. He's driving me nuts."

THIRTY-SIX

The cat was out of the bag sooner than Sam had anticipated. It was mid-March when SAs Cook and Hilton were paid a visit from Trevor Wilson, an IRS agent who worked criminal matters and was stationed in a one-man office in St. George just around the corner from the FBI. All three were good friends who had worked together in the past on cases in which both agencies had jurisdiction.

"Just got some info that may interest you gents," Wilson proudly announced. "Got a call from my supervisor in Salt Lake that he had just been on the phone with our headquarters in Washington concerning one Mr. Samuel P. Donahue." Trevor was being overly formal. They had discussed their mutual interest in the Sam Scam countless times in the past. They potentially shared joint jurisdiction when it came to his alleged crime. Right now, the FBI was taking the lead because the suspected theft was the only known crime. "Would you like to hear more?" Trevor chided. "Wouldn't want to interrupt you if you have something more important going."

"Cut the crap Trev," Tony light heartedly demanded. "Spit it out. What've ya got?"

"Well, it appears our boy transferred just over $900,000 toward the end of January to an account in the Cayman Islands from a Wells Fargo branch in Las Vegas. An auditor was apparently recently looking over the books and reported the transfer as a potentially suspicious transaction. Since I had previously tagged Donahue's name as a person of interest and after working its way up the line, I finally got the call this morning. Not bad, huh?"

"Not bad at all my friend," Tony enthusiastically responded. "I've been telling Steve for some time now I thought you might have some slight potential as an investigator."

"First things first," Steve suggested. "We need to get the ball rolling today and get a subpoena for Wells Fargo from the Assistant United States Attorney to start the trace of the source of the money. I'd like to get the account records from the bank this afternoon if at all possible. Tony, old buddy, I'd appreciate it if you could work on getting the subpoena sooner than later. I've got an interview this morning I can't get out of. Get me the subpoena and I'll head for the bank after lunch."

"No problem, partner. I'll have it in your hands before noon. We've been waiting for this day for too long now. This may be the smoking gun or at least the first step in getting there."

"Don't forget me," Trevor added. "If this turns into money laundering or some other tax violation, we may be working this as a joint task force."

You needn't concern yourself about that, Trev," Steve responded with a slight smirk. "The more the merrier. Our only concern is getting the money back and putting this guy away. You're far better equipped than we are to tackle the tax angle. The more pressure we can bring as a team, the better. Besides, Tony confided in me a while back there was actually a time not that long ago when he actually, sort of, didn't mind all that much, on a rare occasion, working with you."

"That's bull," Tony protested. "I'd never admit to anything like that."

Without completely neglecting the rest of their caseloads, it took Steve and Tony the better part of a month to piece together the source of the overseas transfer. After getting the subpoena to obtain Sam's account records at Wells Fargo, they had to return to the AUSA to get subpoenas for all the banks disclosing deposits into his account. From there, they had to return yet again to get even more subpoenas for all the casinos from which he had initially obtained checks to make the deposits.

This initial stage of tracking the money ended up with a large investigative wall chart depicting 156 casinos with total winnings exceeding 1.5 million dollars. They needed more help to hand out the subpoenas and conduct multiple interviews at each of the casinos. Both headquarters in Salt Lake and Las Vegas agreed to provide two additional agents each to help canvas the casinos. Steve prepared a set of instructions and a list of questions that needed to be answered. The casinos were divided up evenly so each agent was responsible for twenty six of the total.

The information on the instruction and question sheet included: (1) Determine the source and amount of funds used by Donahue to purchase gambling chips. Obtain all paperwork including receipts reflecting such purchases. (2) Identify and interview employees at teller cages and gaming tables who recall dealing with Donahue as a player. Determine if he was generally a loser or a winner and if he was capable of winning large amounts of money. Use attached photo of him to help in employee identification. (3) Contact security to see if he had been targeted in anyway because of his possible exceptional play. (4) Conduct any follow-up investigation deemed necessary based on results of 1-3.

Included as part of the instructions, Steve made it clear what the general purpose of the leads entailed, since some of the agents hadn't worked these type of cases before. He briefly summarized the theory of laundering illegal funds when it came to using casinos. He explained that launderers like Donahue purchased chips under the pretense of gambling. In reality, they bet very little while cashing in the vast majority of chips to obtain laundered cash that could be claimed as gaming proceeds.

Proving that the cashed in chips that didn't come from winning at blackjack would show his gain came from a source other than gambling. Without any other explanation for the extra cash, which didn't appear to now exist, the stolen funds from the armored car would be the logical source of chip yield and would most likely provide the lynchpin to convince a jury of his guilt. Steve reminded the lead agents how close the total deposits were to the amount stolen in the heist. How could someone like Donahue come up with that much money if it could be proven, by these interviews, it didn't come from luck at the gambling table?

It didn't take long for Sam to discover the multitude of interviews being conducted on his behalf. Although being asked to keep the inquiries confidential, dozens of casino employees had immediately pulled him aside to warn him of the full court press. Nothing unexpected. Just a little earlier than he had planned for. Still, the master plan was fundamentally unaffected. Things were proceeding almost precisely along the path he had so carefully designed.

THIRTY-SEVEN

The cadre of agents were still interviewing casino employees when Sam filed his 2015 tax return by placing it in the drop-off box at the St. George Post Office late Thursday, April 14th. Now in the final stages of his astonishingly successful, so far, master plan, he relaxed by proceeding straight to the local golf course where he was lucky enough to team up with a tanned beauty in tight jeans who, as luck would have it, happened to have also arrived at the course solo. Not only good looking, but a talented golfer to boot, he savored a competitive and visibly invigorating 18 holes.

The tax return was straight forward and easy to fill out. His income included wages prior to being fired, unemployment benefits afterwards and some interest on his bank accounts. He took a standard deduction. On line 21 of his 1040, however, under "other income", he included an amount that would separate his return from the rest. He showed $1,680,000 identified as net gambling winnings. He included a check payable to the IRS for $581, 640. The winnings closely matched the total of the deposits from checks issued from the 150 casinos.

Copies of all the cancelled checks currently being gathered by the agents would actually end up exceeding the amount identified as net winnings. That was because he had deducted the purchase of receipted chips toward the end after all his stolen money had been laundered. After all the auditing, one violation IRS SA Wilson would not be investigating was his failure to pay taxes on his income. Some IRS auditor might question why he hadn't reduced his tax burden by reporting more loses he had to have incurred. But, in the end, any such loses would have only justified a reduction in the amount owed. The IRS wasn't going to argue about that.

There would be little doubt in the flummoxed minds of the FBI as to why he had intentionally increased his tax liability by failing to disclose the amount he had invested in chips. Divulging what he had actually wagered would have disclosed his alleged winnings were bogus consisting primarily of the stolen funds. What was obvious to the investigators, however, might prove less convincing to jurors; especially, if such a panel was expertly influenced by a topnotch defense attorney. After all, could it be proven beyond a reasonable doubt a gambler couldn't win big? It was rare, but the possibility couldn't be entirely brushed aside.

To make any successful prosecution even more unlikely, lead agents were currently in the process of determining he had the reputation of being a uniquely superior gambler. Although the majority of his time at the tables had occurred in disguise mode, it now appeared he had in his undisguised persona garnered a sufficient number of credible witnesses who could verify his exceptional ability. Steve and Tony were quickly approaching the disheartening realization such witnesses could and most likely would prove to be a formable barrier in any attempt at a successful prosecution.

He was confident it wouldn't be necessary, but in case it was, he was willing to fully expose his ability to win big. If it ultimately became iffy a jury might not accept that possibility, he would fully disclose his use of disguises and exceptional card playing skills. The fact casino security for the most part had been unable to catch him card counting was what had precipitated his atypical success.

Before worrying about what a jury might think, SAs Cook and Hilton would have to convince AUSA Samuelson to take the case to a grand jury to seek an indictment. Although it wasn't that difficult to get such a body, unfairly influenced by the prosecution, to indict, any AUSA worth his/her salt knew it was quite another matter to win a case in front of a jury. Unless you wanted to be known as a loser, the prosecution better have its ducks in a row before considering the relatively easier initial step of obtaining an indictment.

It's not unusual for investigators to consider the evidence sufficient to convict while prosecutors are far more reluctant to proceed. That's because the prosecutor has extensive experience in facing wily defense attorneys and what it takes to convince an unpredictable panel of jurors. Prosecutors are often seen by short-sighted investigators as being overly cautious by demanding additional investigation to provide more supporting evidence before they will consider moving forward.

In the past, a strong working relationship between FBI case agents and AUSAs had proven problematic. Before his death in 1972, J. Edgar Hoover had made it clear he didn't want his agents being controlled by prosecutors. As a result, some agents took that to mean they determined what and how much investigation needed to be conducted. Once they turned over their final investigative report, they were sometimes unreasonably reluctant to respond to the complaints of an AUSA that their investigative efforts had fallen short.

Luckily, that stubborn mind set had slowly been replaced by the wiser course of seeking to incorporate the suggestions of prosecutors from the beginning. More agents acknowledged the benefit of welcoming the investigative advice of those who would be charged with proving a case in the courtroom. Working together as a team against the bad guys was far more productive than concentrating on who might be encroaching on each other's turf. That was the kind of relationship Steve and Tony enjoyed with AUSA Samuelson.

It was because of that close bond they would not pressure Samuelson to indict unless he felt confident he could successfully prosecute Sam and obtain a guilty verdict by a jury of his peers. Even though both SAs felt heartened about the discovery of the overseas transfer and what it might finally mean to the successful outcome of the case, they weren't about to claim victory quite yet. The transfer seemed a little too transparent for someone that cagy. Would the apparently obvious source of the transfer be yet another example in a string of hopeful developments followed by squelched disappointments?

THIRTY-EIGHT

Spring 2016 had run its course and the stifling heat of the approaching summer was rapidly emerging. Forecasters were predicting more record breaking high temperatures. Some claimed it was further proof of global warming. With a larger number of tea party enthusiasts in the St. George area, most local residents refuted that analysis and pointed to isolated years in the distant past when temperatures had been even higher.

One thing for sure was the climate in Las Vegas would soon turn woeful, nothing unusual. It was always wretchedly hot by the time June arrived. Las Vegas most probably wouldn't exist in its present state if it wasn't for air conditioning. Luckily for Sam, most of the time he spent there was in the moderating confines of casinos and swimming pools. The cost of coolness was astronomically high, but easily covered by the vast preponderance of losers who carelessly bet their savings with little chance of cashing in. He wasn't one of them.

He was one of the gifted few who had figured a way to legally game the system. He was enjoying all the perks offered to those who were willing to risk their luck on a regular basis. His biggest concern was being rejected if it was determined he was counting cards. So far, cross his fingers, with a couple of exceptions, none of the other casinos had approached him with an invitation to take his unwelcome skills elsewhere.

He had slowly come to the realization he could legitimately earn a fairly decent living at the blackjack tables. If it ended up he might become targeted for expulsion using his true identity, he figured he could go back to using disguises. He could see no way he could be stopped if it came to that. He would simply return to his practice of buying chips with cash in relatively small amounts with no record of the purchase. By the time he cashed in his chips, it would be highly unlikely his good fortune could be tied directly to his surreptitious play. Yeah, his taxes would be higher without being able to counterbalance winnings with losses, but big deal. Just a minor glitch. Nothing more than an irritating expense of doing business.

Perhaps, if he had earlier grasped his overwhelming talent as a player, he might not have stolen the money. He now realized he could in all probability have enjoyed a fairly decent lifestyle with only the need to avail himself of initial cash withdrawals on his credit cards to get started. Too late to worry about what might have been. There was no turning back the clock. As long as he didn't get caught, he had a reserve fund exceeding well over a million dollars to help provide additional economic stability. The future could never be considered absolutely secure. Unforeseen adverse occurrences could always come to pass. A substantial buffer fund still made the heist a wise decision.

One thing he wouldn't do would be to risk his ill-gotten gain on the blackjack tables. He was anything but a compulsive gambler. Although confident in his ability to win, he also realized the wisdom in not jeopardizing everything as so many gamblers do. He had already risked the chance of going to jail. He would be especially cautious to disengage from the multitude of unsound blackjack scenarios that might risk the newfound wealth he had worked so long and hard to achieve.

As one final precaution, should he ever be forced to face a trial, he might require a healthy cash reserve for decent legal representation. That better never happen. All his effort could be for naught with a possible conviction and all the obvious downside that would entail. Still, you could never tell about a complex jury. Not to worry. Trying to objectively evaluate his present situation from every angle, he felt practically zero concern at this late stage of his carefully crafted scheme.

The time had arrived to face the music. The lead agents had finally completed their interviews at the multitude of casinos. All the possible evidence had been compiled. There was no more waiting to catch him cashing in on the stolen funds. The location of the money had now been identified. Everything concerning his potential guilt was laid bare in the tall stack of investigative reports resting on the desk of AUSA Samuelson back to work and feeling well again. Sitting across from him were SAs Cook and Lytle intently engaged in an intensive discussion with the purpose of obtaining a final prosecutive opinion.

"Unless I've missed something, I don't see where all the casino interviews have come up with any kind of smoking gun," Samuelson glumly observed. "There appears to be no evidence indicating that Donahue ever purchased 1.5 million of chips in an effort to launder the theft. We have no way of proving beyond a reasonable doubt he purchased far fewer chips with his relatively meager sources of income and won big, exceptionally big. There seems to be no record of how many chips he may have actually purchased.

"Worse than that," SA Cook reluctantly lamented. "The interviews have resulted in few employees who could identify him as a player when shown his picture. Those who did know him well describe him as a gifted player who has the potential to win big in spite of not being able to personally recall him ever winning that much. Then, there are the officials at the Excalibur who banned him from further play for being suspected as a card counter. That bolsters even further an extraordinary ability to win."

"Yeah, I noticed all that. Not too helpful to say the least," Samuelson agreed. "Not only can't we prove to a jury he washed the money, but there appear to be several potential credible witnesses for the defense who could convincingly support the real possibility, as slight as it might seem, he could have potentially won such a bonanza fair and square. Never mind the amount won is suspiciously similar to the amount stolen. I can't see any other investigative results to impress a grand jury, much less a regular jury, he did the dirty deed. Have I missed something? If not, I'm not willing to present this case for indictment as things now stand."

"As much as it irks us," Steve reluctantly responded, "we've tried about every investigatory technique we can think of. I can appreciate your hesitancy to proceed. I think Tony joins me in agreeing you may have no other viable option for the time being other than to decline prosecution. We'll place the matter in a pending-inactive status. Since we know he's guilty, we're not going to close the case entirely. To be honest about it, about the only chance we have left is if he ever confides in others about what he did and they contact us and we can prove such an admission of guilt took place."

"Sounds good to me," Samuelson concluded trying to end on a hopeful tone. "You get me even one reliable witness like that and I'll indict the smug bastard in a heartbeat. That might be all we need as far as I'm concerned. All the other circumstantial evidence we already have with even one witness like that would in all probability get the job done. Of course, to state the obvious, we would have to convince a jury beyond a reasonable doubt any such witness was telling the truth. Good luck!"

THIRTY-NINE

Transferring the majority of Sam's ill-gotten booty from the U.S. to Grand Cayman was done with the intention of making it more difficult for law enforcement to place a hold in the unlikely event it was decided to push forward with an indictment. Unlikely, because Sam was confident law enforcement was currently incapable of convincing a prosecutor his alleged winnings at the blackjack tables weren't bona fide. Nevertheless, in his way of thinking, a credible master plan didn't deserve the title if not covering every conceivable contingency.

Although some strides over the years had been made to cooperate with U.S. investigators concerning off-shore money laundering and other substantial criminal misconduct, these agreements made it clear the cooperation was based on furnishing convincing evidence of illegality before any sensitive banking information would be shared. After all, it was estimated that up to one-third of GDP in the Cayman Islands was based on financial services touted as providing confidentiality and tax advantage.

Since there was currently insufficient probable cause to prove he had laundered funds through the casinos, the policy of law enforcement in Grand Cayman would most likely be to refuse to cooperate with any effort by U.S. authorities to delve into his current bank account or any financial transactions emanating therefrom. That, at least, was the reaction he hoped for should any such attempt materialize.

It was now over three months since he had filed his tax return in which he disclosed his alleged gambling income. He had become convinced he was no longer being followed and it appeared he was no longer being actively investigated. None of his friends and associates had reported any further contact by the FBI or anyone else interested in the robbery. He thought it was somewhat premature to give up that easily, but that's exactly what appeared to have happened. He decided it was about time to take a trip to Grand Cayman for a Caribbean splash of both business and pleasure.

He had transferred the $900,000 to the Cayman National Bank in the George Town section of Grand Cayman. Just to be extra cautious, the day after arriving, he closed the account and transferred half that amount to the Bank Vontobel and the other half to Banko DoBrazil, both located nearby. A few days later, he closed both those accounts and transferred the entire amount to Banco BCN, also locally situated. The reasoning behind the additional movement was to add a couple more layers of cover.

The reason for making the last stop at Banco BCN was a tip from a fellow gambler back in Las Vegas about a particular banking official there who had a reputation of being particularly protective of customer deposits. It was even rumored this individual may be willing to consider steps to cautiously but effectively sidetrack existing law between the U.S. and Grand Cayman if he was to receive a reasonable personal service fee for his willingness to look the other way.

He discovered the bank official by the name of Ernesto Alvarez to be not all that discreet after joining him at a local bar for a couple drinks. He readily ensured Sam's privacy regardless of existing regulations for $10,000 cash. Sam agreed based on the fact the banker had as much to lose if not more if the bribe ever came to light. He withdrew the cash the next day and cautiously passed it to Ernesto in an anonymous white envelope while sitting at his desk in the bank.

Just like he did with all his bank accounts, he memorized his account number and made sure he never had any documentation in his possession that could provide a paper trail to his financial activities. He had no trouble quickly memorizing lists of numbers and recalling them. Not that it really mattered anymore since there was nothing illegal that could be tied to the account, but why not take advantage of his unique talent as an added level of anonymity?

Now came the relaxation part. Sam didn't hesitate when Ernesto offered to arrange for free golf on the tab of the bank at the premier golf course in Grand Cayman. Not for just one round, but a free pass for the remainder of the month. Sam had recently signed up as a Marriott time-share owner and had already opted for a two week stay at a luxurious Marriott Resort on Seven Mile Beach. The golf course was conveniently situated nearby.

The North Sound Golf Club was designed by Englishman Roy Case in 1994. It was the only local 18 hole layout on the island styled in the traditional Scottish link format with beautifully manicured fairways, powdery pure white sandy bunkers, and surrounded by gorgeous ocean views; a golfer's paradise to brag about with his golf buddies back home for years to come.

He had been having trouble with his King Cobra 9.5 degree driver. Although most of his drives off the tee box were fairly long, over 200 yards and most within the bounds of the fairway, he had recently developed the bad habit of either pulling sharply to the left or sending some high to the right on enough instances to cause him concern. He decided his goal over the next couple of weeks would be to become more consistent. His first attempt at a solution was to take a couple of lessons from the course pro. Armed with the opinion he needed to improve the timing of his wrist turn and follow-through, Sam decided to take full advantage of his free play.

Using a cart to help temper physical fatigue, he began playing 36 holes/day and was almost immediately rewarded with a significant improvement in his ability to consistently strike his drives longer and more accurately. He planned to surprise those cocky players back home who had heretofore considered him somewhat susceptible when it came to friendly wagers. Actually, winning or losing money was secondary. He just loved the competition and bragging rights.

Golf was a humbling game and anyone with an overabundant ego would probably be well advised to find an alternative sport. His admittedly significant ego, however, didn't translate into considering even for a moment the option of abandoning the sport he so thoroughly coveted. The same DNA that drove him to consider every possible aspect of his master plan drove his desire to improve his golf game. Just like perfecting his blackjack playing ability, honing his ability on the links was an ever present motivation.

Relaxing with a cold frosted mug of Sam Adams in the plush club lounge following an especially satisfying day of golf, he caught the eye of scrumptious blond who he thought for a moment might be eying him from across the bar. After catching her one more time appearing to smile in his direction, he didn't hesitate to slightly raise his frosted mug in return while flashing his perfect set of pearly-whites that had served him so well in the past.

FORTY

The worry of being caught was no longer a concern. The master plan had worked to perfection. Sam felt untouchable and downright giddy now every potential barrier to success had been ingeniously eliminated. It had been approaching just over a year and a half since the robbery, sooner than he had originally anticipated even under the most favorable of circumstances.

Grand Cayman was exquisite, the golf exceptional and his second frosted mug of beer especially refreshing. The blond across the way was looking really good. He couldn't remember the last time he felt that horny. He suspected the complete lack of any further peripheral anxiety probably had something to do with it.

Her name was Kathy. She was two years younger than him, stunning in appearance and could easily be mistaken for a movie star. She was a successful golfer and member of the Ladies Professional Golf Association. She was currently ranked 20th on the LPGA tour with earnings so far this year of just over $90,000. She lived in Phoenix and was taking a break in Grand Cayman following a fifteenth place finish in her last tournament.

They didn't waste any time in engaging in their initial sexual encounter. There was no doubt about the intense physical attraction each had for the other. But it was more than that. Not since Mandy had he felt so at ease with a woman. She was brilliant and both shared the same interests and curiosities. Add that to her obvious enthusiasm for golf and he was rapidly considering a more permanent relationship. Why not? He was no longer preoccupied with the master plan.

He could visualize the amazing relationship they could experience together. She had been divorced, but had no children or any other baggage to get in the way. Both decided to extend their stay on the island for an additional two weeks to get to know each other better. It became obvious into the second week her answer was going to be resoundingly in the affirmative if he popped the question and that was exactly what he had finally determined to do.

Not that it made that much difference, but financial security was an added bonus. He could see himself accompanying her on the tour and playing some of the best courses together for the foreseeable future. She already knew he was a millionaire and believed him when he informed her of his gambling expertise. He would make sure he provided more than his fair share of marital expenses. He would assure her he was more than willing to sign a prenup to protect her assets or not. It would be her choice. Divorce wasn't in his plans. He was that sure about their compatibility.

He purchased the ring and determined to ask her to marry him following a round of golf together on the night before both had scheduled to return home. He couldn't help reflect on the change his life had taken from when he first began planning the armored car heist. All the countless hours of preparation and execution had finally paid off. No longer was he tied to the monotony and frustration of his previous dead end employment. His health was exceptional and he was playing golf with the love of his life on an island paradise. The only pressure he faced was improving his chipping and putting.

The big day was exquisite. His plan was to present the ring on the 18th green after they had completed their round. The weather was cooperating beautifully with practically no bothersome wind, just a gentle tropical breeze that helped minimize the heat of the sun. The sky was bright blue with a few brilliantly white puffy clouds providing a stark contrast. She was dressed to kill in her short golf skirt and sleeveless top. What incredible shoulders and legs! This was destined to be a romantic interlude with no end in sight.

It happened on the 17th hole. It was so sudden it didn't seem real. Sam was lying face down near the 150 yard marker. Someone from the adjoining fairway had yelled "four", but it had been too late. The small white Titleist Pro V1x had apparently struck him somewhere that had caused him to immediately fall to the ground. The apologetic golfer who had struck the wayward projectile came running to the scene and frantically dialed 911 when it became apparent he wasn't getting up.

Kathy collapsed as the paramedics declared Sam dead at the scene of the tragic accident. A subsequent autopsy would confirm he had most probably died instantly when the golf ball struck him on his left temple while traveling at a ridiculously high rate of speed. He most undoubtedly hadn't felt a thing.

Son of a bitch! He hadn't figured into his master plan a solution to being hit in the temple by a wayward golf ball. A significant omission as it turned out. Who could have guessed?

THE BITTER END

EPILOGUE

The funeral was well attended considering Sam had no family. The majority of attendees consisted of Las Vegas casino workers. Kathy had talked enough with her deceased lover about his background to realize Las Vegas, not St George, was the logical location. She had arranged the trip home and paid for all the expenses including a follow-up brunch afterwards for everybody who had bothered to read the brief obituary and attend along with others who found out by word of mouth.

Somebody had called the FBI and both SAs Cook and Lytle had attended the solemn proceeding. It was obvious Kathy was heartbroken. The ring had been found in Sam's pocket and she was devastated to find out what may have been. The two agents took the opportunity to tactfully set up an appointment with her for the next day before her plane was scheduled to fly back to her home base in Arizona.

The interview took place in Kathy's room at the Bellagio several hours prior to her scheduled departure. They were skeptical at first but finally came to the conclusion she was being truthful when she told them she and Sam had never discussed details about his assets including where they may be currently ensconced. The only thing he had confided in her was he had close to a million dollars at his disposal due most entirely to his expertise as a card counter at the blackjack tables.

She was shocked when she was asked if he had ever hinted the source of his money was actually tied to an armored car theft. After they explained their suspicion, she seemed bewildered and said she could not believe the man she loved could have ever been involved in such a crime. The interview concluded with the investigators gaining nothing of value from Sam's latest conquest. Boy, you had to hand it to the guy. He knew how to attract them up to the very end. She may qualify as having been the most gorgeous example of the female sex yet.

His bounty was still languishing at the Banco BCN in Grand Cayman almost two months now since his death. Ernesto Alvarez was keeping a close eye on the account in case someone showed up to claim it. Nobody had so far and he wasn't about to report its existence to the authorities. Because of the ten thousand dollar payoff, he suspected the possibility that no one but Sam was aware of the account's existence.

So, after a few more weeks, Ernesto worked his dishonest magic and transferred the money to a phony account while forging Sam's signature and acting as the bank officer who had approved the transfer. The likelihood of anyone ever investigating and determining he had died before the date of the forgery was infinitesimal. After the next bank audit proved that likelihood justified, Mr. Alvarez retired and lived out the remainder of his sleazy existence in unscrupulous luxury.

Since he hadn't been able to benefit, one had to wonder if he would have been happy to know a fellow crook had benefitted from his brilliantly conceived and executed master plan. Sam hadn't been a complete loser. He had thoroughly enjoyed the ride up till the tragic conclusion. The unsuccessful result of his brilliant conniving brings to mind the following famous Aesop fable penned way back in about 570 B.C. entitled "The Milkmaid and Her Pail:"

"Patty, a farmer's daughter, is daydreaming as she walks to town with a pail of milk balanced on her head. Her thoughts: 'The milk in this pail will provide me with cream, which I will make into butter, which I will sell in the market, and buy a dozen eggs, which will hatch into chickens, which will lay more eggs, and soon I'll shall have a large poultry yard. I'll sell some of the fowls and buy myself a handsome new gown and go to the fair, and when the young fellows try to make love to me, I'll toss my head and pass them by.' At that moment, Patty tossed her head and lost the pail full of milk. Her mother admonished, 'do not count your chickens before they are hatched'."

Perhaps that should be a constant reminder for any master planner no matter how ingeniously conceived and executed the scheme.

Printed in the United States
By Bookmasters

Printed in the United States
By Bookmasters